"White men," the dying woman murmured. "Took our children. Took them to be slaves. Shot my husband when he fought back. Shot me when they tried to rape me and I fought them with a knife."

She tried to raise her head again, to look for her children, Gabe supposed. Then a great gout of blood burst from her mouth, and she fell back again, dead.

Gabe slowly stood up. What was the matter with this land? His own land was not a soft one, but this apparent paradise was the most vicious place he'd ever seen. He felt rage stirring within him, but controlled it, let it solidify into a cold, implacable desire—for justice . . .

LONG RIDER

DEAD AIM

CLAY DAWSON

DIAMOND BOOKS, NEW YORK

This book is a Diamond original edition,
and has never been previously published.

DEAD AIM

A Diamond Book/published by arrangement with
the author

PRINTING HISTORY
Diamond edition/July 1993

ISBN: 1-55773-919-6

Diamond Books are published by The Berkley Publishing Group,
200 Madison Avenue, New York, NY 10016.
The name "DIAMOND" and its logo
are trademarks belonging to Charter Communications, Inc.

PRINTED IN THE UNITED STATES OF AMERICA

10 9 8 7 6 5 4 3 2 1

LONG RIDER

★ DEAD AIM ★

CHAPTER ONE

Long Rider was surprised when he awoke; he had not really meant to fall asleep. He lay quietly for several minutes, secure in the warmth and smell of the big buffalo robe, which was a little ripe now after the long winter. But still, the robe was comforting, familiar. He let his mind drift, grabbing at snatches of half-remembered dreams. All he really had left of the dreams were feelings. Of freedom. Of travel. Of vast spaces, towering mountains.

It was then that he finally decided he would go, that it was time to leave. For days he had been struggling with the idea, its good side, its bad side. The bad was leaving the People. What was left of them. The good was getting away from the reservation, from this vast prison.

He quietly slipped out of the bedroll and began wrapping his breechclout around his loins, trying not to wake Running Bear, who lay a few feet away, on the far side of the lodge, sleeping with his wife, Antelope Woman. But Running Bear, sleeping a warrior's light sleep, heard him. The lodge fire had burned down to coals, but there was still enough light for Long Rider to see the slight gleam reflected in Running Bear's open eyes.

Long Rider was collecting his gear. "So," Running Bear said. "You really are leaving, then."

"Yes."

A silence followed. "Ah," Running Bear breathed softly. "If I could only go with you."

Long Rider said nothing. He felt ashamed. Ashamed that he could go and that Running Bear could not. But he must go, he would have to forget his bad feeling, for if he did not leave, he knew he would go mad.

Carrying some of his gear, he left the lodge. He stopped just outside the entrance, listening to the night, as a warrior should. There were no sounds that did not belong, only the sounds of a Lakota village. The sudden barking of a dog in response to the distant wail of a coyote. A murmur of conversation from a lodge, someone else not asleep. He thought he heard, from two lodges away, the whimpering cry of a woman making love. Yes. From Red Buffalo's lodge. Long Rider smiled. Red Buffalo was newly married. For days he and his woman had been keeping half the camp awake.

Long Rider went to the horse herd. A sleepy boy kept guard. He murmured something as Long Rider took one of his horses from the herd, a sturdy little Plains pony, a quiet horse, one that would make a good pack animal. Long Rider spent the next few minutes strapping on an improvised packsaddle, like the kind the White Man used. It took two more trips to the lodge before he had collected all he wanted to take with him. Long Rider smiled wryly. He was getting as bad as the White Man, taking so many things. But who knew when he would be back? If ever.

On his final trip to the lodge, Long Rider picked up his big buffalo-hide coat. In the dim light he could barely make out the design painted high across the back . . . the spread wings of *Wakinyan,* the one the White Man called the Thunderbird. Long Rider slipped his arms into the coat's sleeves. The weight, the warmth of it felt good. Even though it was spring, there was still a nip in the air. More importantly, he felt reassured knowing that *Wakinyan's* protective wings once more lay spread out across his back and shoulders.

Running Bear was sitting up now. Next to him, his wife stirred in her sleep. A satisfied woman. Earlier, Long Rider had listened to the two of them make love. Now Long Rider turned toward Running Bear. "My horses are now your horses."

Politely looking down at the ground, eyes averted, Running Bear nodded his thanks. "Hah!" he burst out. "If I could only . . ."

Long Rider did not reply. He picked up his gun belt and holster and fastened the belt around his bare waist. He wore the holster cavalry style, with the pistol high on the right hip, butt forward. The pistol itself felt satisfyingly heavy. Long Rider saw that Running Bear was looking intently at the pistol. "Count coup for me!" Running Bear said fiercely.

Long Rider felt a lump rise in his throat. "I will," he murmured thickly. Picking up his two rifles, he abruptly left the lodge. Outside, he stopped, looking around the sleeping village, only a few lodges now, a ragged, poor camp. For the People could no longer hunt the buffalo, from which their entire wealth derived. No more buffalo hides to make new lodges, clothing, cooking pouches. No buffalo bones for tools and implements. Not even buffalo chips for fuel. Worst of all, no buffalo meat. The White Man had taken everything, the animals, even the land, and had locked the People up, here in this little corner of the vast territory over which they had ridden free for more lifetimes than could be imagined.

But even as ragged a village as it was, Long Rider drank in its sounds and smells . . . the odor of a dying fire, of stew still giving off a rich aroma; they had killed a cow yesterday, one of the scrawny animals the Agent had given them, with its tasteless meat. But still, meat. They'd had little of that lately.

Long Rider shook his head. Although this village might be very poor, it was still a village of the People, of his Oglala. More than any sound or smell, the sense of the People still lay around him. The warmth of belonging, This, more than anything else, tugged at him, made him wonder if, after all, he should leave. . . .

Do I really belong? he asked himself bitterly. He felt the weight, the confusion, of living somewhere between two worlds, the white world and the world of the People. No, he warned himself, do not confuse yourself. You simply want to leave, you want to ride free, as the People have always ridden free. And what makes you feel bad is that you know that you alone can do this. But, as for the rest, they will remain locked up here. . . .

He went back to the horse herd. His favorite riding horse, the huge black stallion that he had brought back from his last visit to the white world, tried to hide in the middle of the herd. Too much time had passed since the animal had been ridden; it had grown lazy. Long Rider had to loop a rope around the stallion's neck, then tug it out of the herd. But once out by itself, the stallion seemed to grow more interested in what might lie ahead. It took Long Rider only a short time to put the woven horsehair bridle in place. Picking up his Winchester, he led both horses toward the edge of the village.

There was a bright moon; he could see over the prairie for some distance. A stream lay less than a hundred yards away. He led the horses there, wanting them to drink well before they started out over the vastness of the prairie. The horses, smelling the water, went willingly enough. When they reached the stream, Long Rider crouched down on his heels, to fill a pouch with water for himself, while the horses drank. The pouch was almost full when he heard a sound behind him, a soft step, the rustling of clothing. He dropped the pouch, reached across with his left hand, pulled out the pistol, and cranked back the hammer while he spun around on his heels, all in one motion.

"Oh!" a voice burst out. A girl's voice, frightened. Long Rider relaxed, seeing that it was only Two Rivers, Running Bear's younger sister. He eased down the pistol's hammer. "You should not walk up behind a man that way," he said gruffly, partly to conceal his embarrassment.

The girl stood silent and straight, hands clasped in front of her, head down. "You are leaving, then," she said softly. "You have decided."

Long Rider was aware of the sadness in the girl's voice. He had been aware for some time how she looked at him, how her eyes followed him everywhere. If he had not already been thinking of leaving, he might have been more interested. Two Rivers was a lovely girl, with huge dark eyes and a strong, lithe body. Long Rider thought she must be about seventeen. He'd wondered at first why no man had as yet married her . . . until he remembered there were few men left. The soldiers had killed so many.

"Yes," Long Rider finally said to the girl. "I am leaving."

Two Rivers raised her head. "And you will not return," she said. It was a statement, not a question.

Long Rider shrugged. "I do not know. But I will ride far."

Two Rivers raised her head, looked straight at him for a moment, uncharacteristic of the girl. Her head dropped again, and when she spoke, her voice was so soft he could barely hear the words. "Perhaps . . . before you leave," she said, "you . . . you could lie with me. Make me your woman . . . if only for a little while."

Long Rider was startled, but not completely surprised. If he had not been so wrapped up in the question of whether or not he should leave the People, what she now wanted would probably already have taken place. He knew that Running Bear had wanted it, had wanted his friend to join with his sister.

It had been a while since Long Rider had had a woman. He now became intensely aware of Two Rivers's loveliness. He also remembered that it was that loveliness that had kept him from becoming closer to her. She looked too much like his wife, Yellow Buckskin Girl. His dead wife. Too many times, when he had come upon Two Rivers, he had been reminded of Yellow Buckskin Girl. Reminded of how he had watched, helpless, as Captain Price's bullet had torn a hole in Yellow Buckskin Girl's forehead. How she had died in front of him.

But now, here by the stream, as he was getting ready to ride away from the village, he began to see Two Rivers as herself. As a beautiful young woman, standing straight in the moonlight, her two braids hanging inky black over the tight swell of her breasts, which were clearly rising and falling rapidly beneath the soft covering of deerskin that hid them.

Long Rider felt himself becoming aroused. He rose to his feet in one smooth motion. When he took the girl in his arms, he could feel her trembling. Not from fear, she was no virgin, he knew that, had heard a couple of the young men talking about her. No, she was trembling from excitement.

He reached down, to lift her dress over her head. He could hear her rapid breathing as she reached out to help when the dress caught on the underside of her breasts. Then she was naked, her flesh gleaming in the moonlight. He took a moment to study the girl, to look at her breasts, full and high, the intake of her taut belly, the shadowed patch between her thighs, the sleekness of the legs below. And the loveliness of her face, the soft skin, the full lips and dark eyes, close now, as Gabe pressed the girl against him.

He suddenly stepped back, shrugged out of the coat, fumbled with his breechclout, let both drop to the ground. Now, as naked as she was, he pressed himself to her once again, marveling at the heat and softness of her body.

They made love on the soft grass, next to the stream. It was short, wild, but also with an overlay of tenderness. Her cries of pleasure floated away on the night air to mingle with the other night sounds. Then for a time afterward, everything was hushed and silent around them.

Long Rider held the girl for a little while longer, then slowly rolled free. She remained lying on her back, looking up at him. "I will hope," she said, "that you have given me a baby. Given me a part of you that I may keep. A part of you that will stay here, with the People."

"I would be happy if that happens . . . has happened," Long Rider said softly. He hesitated a moment. "Two Rivers," he said softly, "your memory will ride with me."

They did not have much to say after that. Long Rider, after a moment's searching, found his breechclout and coat, and put them on. Two Rivers got up, but did not put on her dress. She stood naked in the moonlight, like a spirit-woman, while Long Rider went over to his two horses. She watched as he picked up his rifle and leaped onto the black stallion's broad back. He sat silently for a moment, a tall figure on a tall horse, looking down at Two Rivers. She stepped forward, took the packhorse's halter and handed it up to him. For just a moment their hands touched.

He started to leave, but when he was only a few yards away, he twisted around on the stallion's back and looked at Two Rivers. She was still standing naked, watching him. She did not wave, nor did he. Their leave-taking was completed in silence. But the silence did not make that leave-taking any less intense. With an effort, Long Rider tore his gaze away, then dug his heels into the black stallion's side. What was done was done.

CHAPTER TWO

He had ridden for only a few hours when, over his left shoulder, the sky began to lighten. He rode for another hour, watching the prairie appear around him, revealed by the growing light. The prairie over which he'd ridden since before he'd been old enough to walk. As a baby, each time the People moved, he'd been perched up on one of the horses dragging a travois. And the People had moved often. Now, a grown man, he was still riding that prairie, that vastness, that sea of grass, green now after the spring rains. He looked out over the prairie's immensity. It stretched away and away and away toward a distant, hazy horizon.

He rode easily, without too much worry. He was still on the reservation. There was not much chance of meeting hostile Crow or Pawnee; they were cooped up on their own reservations. Nor was there much chance of meeting hostile whites. They were not supposed to come onto Lakota lands, although some did, illegally, usually to trade alcohol or shoddy goods with the reservation's captives.

Reservation. How he hated the sound of it, the very implication of the word, as if it implied a gift, land "reserved" for the heathen Indian. Reserved out of the vast lands the whites had stolen from the tribes. When Long Rider had been a boy, the Oglala had ridden over a vast area, from what the whites now called the Dakotas, as far south as

Colorado, and from the eastern edges of the Great Plains, west to the Rockies. And now this once free people were penned up in the western part of the Dakota territory. Even so, many whites felt it was still too much land for them, that it could better be used for grazing their cattle, animals that destroyed the grass. Worse, animals whose meat had almost no taste.

Well, he was free. He would ride wherever he wanted to ride. He still felt guilty about leaving the others behind; they could not travel as he could travel. But why stay? There was no fighting now; they did not really need him. Now that the tribe was reduced to living off the scrawny cattle provided by the government, the few the crooked Indian Agents did not steal, he was just one more mouth to feed.

Before, it had been a different matter. Long Rider lost himself in memories of the fighting, when he had ridden under Red Cloud's leadership. A great warrior, Red Cloud, a warrior who had beaten the white soldiers, who had forced them to leave Lakota land. At least for a while. Even the whites called him a great general.

Long Rider remembered the hard fights, the days and nights when he'd ridden beside another great man, his friend, Crazy Horse, a man of visions, a man who lived half in the spirit world. It had been good fighting, and fighting was a warrior's life. But in the end, it had been a losing fight.

Then, the pressure to move onto reservations, the resistance . . . until Red Cloud himself traveled East, to meet with the President, Red Cloud's amazement on seeing the realities of the white world, white strength. Long Rider himself had seen it himself, earlier, when he'd gone East. Day after day of traveling past white towns and cities, with even the smaller cities having more inhabitants than the combined numbers of all the Lakota. A thousand miles of white cities. Cities from which more soldiers could be drawn to fight the Red Man. Cities capable of producing endless numbers of weapons for those soldiers.

Red Cloud had come back a chastened man. Long Rider had seen it in his face, the knowledge that to fight on would mean the complete extermination of the People. So Red Cloud had gone meekly to the reservation. Long Rider had not agreed. Along with some of the younger men, he'd wanted to fight on. Better to die fighting than to become the White Man's tame dog. That's what they'd thought, those younger men . . . until they'd seen the women and children dying, starving, freezing to death as they fled the relentless pressure of the soldiers.

Enough, Long Rider thought. I will not think of those things anymore. I will enjoy this beautiful day.

It was growing warm now. He took off his Thunderbird coat and tossed it over the pack on the other horse. The sun felt good on his naked torso. A slight breeze had risen. He liked the way it blew his long hair over his shoulders in a gentle, sensual caress, hair against bare skin. He was free, life was once again worth living.

However, there was something he was going to have to take care of soon. The opportunity lay about half a mile ahead, a dark line against the green of the new prairie grass, a line of trees, which meant he would probably find running water there.

All the way to the trees, Long Rider kept to the lowest ground, not that there was much to hide behind on the prairie, but by riding along shallow depressions gouged out by heavy rains, he was able to keep off the skyline most of the time.

He dismounted about a hundred yards from the trees, then walked away from his horses, so their breathing would not intrude on other sounds. He stood for several minutes, observing, listening. The trees were only a thin screen along the narrow channel of a small stream. He could see nothing among them. Which might not mean much. He'd seen as many as a dozen Crow or Pawnee hide in terrain that shouldn't have been able to conceal partridges. And the Crow and Pawnee were old enemies of the Lakota. Many lifetimes ago, according to the old stories, the Lakota had come into the Plains from the east. The Crow had been riding these plains then, lords of all they surveyed. And the Lakota had driven them out, driven them further toward the setting sun. Since then, Crow had hated Lakota, and Lakota had hated Crow. Now that he had lost his own land, Long Rider could understand the bitterness of the Crow Nation. But, justice or not, a Lakota who wanted to stay alive kept his eyes open for his people's old enemies.

Finally, it was the natural behavior of the few birds hopping among the tree branches that convinced Long Rider that there was no one hiding near the stream. Mounting his horse again and leading the packhorse, he rode straight in. Dismounting, he hid his horses as best he could in a patch of brush, then left them cropping grass while he walked down to the stream.

It was a gentle little stream, its width about twice the height of a man, moving sluggishly in a shallow channel. Here and there pools had formed where the channel was deeper. Long Rider headed for one of those pools, dropping his loincloth along the way. He'd been foolish to go this long without washing himself; he should have done it in the stream near the village, immediately after making love to Two Rivers. There might be fighting ahead, who could know for certain? And Long Rider understood, had been taught since boyhood, that a warrior facing battle had to wash himself after making love to a woman. To go into battle impure was a way of courting death; it was an insult to the spirits.

Long Rider smiled bitterly. He knew that most white men would consider such a belief only another example of heathen Indian superstition. Perhaps it was, but Long Rider was not about to take the chance.

It was while he was bending over the little pool of quiet water that Long Rider received the familiar jolt. The surface of the water formed a perfect mirror, and in it, he could see himself. Could see the reflection of his long, sandy-colored hair. Hair that was almost blond. Could see the gray color of his eyes, so light a shade of gray that they were almost colorless. Living among the Lakota, seeing, every day, their dark skin, black hair and eyes, he tended to forget how he himself looked. Yes, his skin was dark, burned by the sun, but it had been burned a golden bronze color, not the darker brown of most of the People. Naked, the area where his loincloth had been was very white.

For he had the body of a white man. Indeed, according to most people, he was a white man.

But my spirit is Lakota! he told himself fiercely. Then he shook his head. No, only half-Lakota.

He stepped into the water, destroying his image. After washing himself thoroughly, he left the water and lay down on the bank to let the warm sun dry his skin. But, restless, he got up and went over to the packhorse. Rummaging through the pack, he brought out a leather-covered book. An old, battered book, which he took back to the bank. Squatting, with the sun hot on his bare shoulders, he opened the book.

It was a Bible. His mother's family Bible. Her name was written in the front of the book, along with other names, including his own. Gabe Conrad. That was his name, the one his mother had written down for him when he'd been born. And her name . . . Amelia Reid. Before she'd married his father, Adam Conrad. All this she had told him, had showed him, too, because she had taught him to read and write the White Man's language from this very book. Amelia Conrad. But he had first known her by the name she was called among the People, Yellow Hair, because her hair had been the color of the yellow metal, the one the whites went crazy over. Hair the color of gold.

He smiled. Her hair, and his own, had given him many worries when he was a boy, because both he and his mother looked so different from all the other Oglala. Few boys like to be different. His mother had reassured him, had even made him a little arrogant for a while, when she had explained that the sun had descended just for them, had touched them both with its golden light, had given them a special sign of its care, in the color of their hair, their eyes.

He turned a few pages. There was writing all along the margins, slanting every which way, as space allowed. Tiny, neat writing. His mother's journal, written down in berry juice, using a pen made from an eagle feather, on the only paper she had.

The journal told her story. How she and her husband had been traveling in a wagon train with other white men, on their way to Oregon. How she and Adam, along with a few others, had left the train when they heard a rumor that there was gold in the Black Hills. How a band of Oglala, the Bad Faces, had discovered them there, profaning a place sacred to the Lakota, and had wiped them out. All except for Amelia. She'd been the last left alive, and had stood, eyes defiant, holding an empty rifle like a club, the body of her dead husband only a few yards away.

Impressed by her bravery, one of the Oglala warriors, Little Wound, had spared her. Had taken her back to the village, where he made her his woman. Which she remained until the day she died, more than twenty years later.

Long Rider had been born nine months after his mother's capture. He smiled as he remembered part of her story, a part that was not written down in the black book. How she and her husband, waking early on the morning of the attack, had made love, how she had gotten pregnant just minutes before the Bad Faces attacked and killed her husband and the others. She had told Long Rider this, had told him, smiling. He knew that she could not have said such a thing if she had stayed among the whites. White women had trouble with such thoughts, but among the Lakota the ways of nature were not something to be ashamed of. Yes, living among the People had changed his mother.

As he sat thinking of his mother, an ugly image wormed its way into his mind. An image of the shining steel of a cavalry saber sinking into her chest. Long Rider immediately suppressed the image. This was not a day to remember old wounds. This was a day to start a new freedom. A day to remember that he had been born among the Lakota, had grown up among the Lakota, indeed, had not thought about being a white man until much, much later. Until he discovered, on his first trip among the whites, that he was a man who lived halfway between two worlds. His mother, teaching him to read out of that Bible, with its words, with its strange values, had also taught him elements of the white way of life. Being young, some of that way had stuck.

Long Rider abruptly stood up. He would ride away from here, this must be a spirit place; something was happening to his mind. Spirits often stayed near water. He would ride out onto the prairie, and there, surrounded by the cleanness of the land, his mind would find peace.

CHAPTER THREE

He rode most of the day, until, in the afternoon, his horses began to tire. He made camp in a small depression, where he and his horses would be concealed, but where he could poke his head above the edge of the depression and see for quite a ways. He did not make a fire; there was nothing to cook. He ate some dried meat he'd brought with him and a little pemmican, washed down with water.

Before it was dark he took his bedroll from his packhorse. The bedroll was one feature of the White Man's world he'd come to value. His was made of some old wool blankets, sewn together, with loose wool stuffed in between the blanket layers. The night was fairly warm, so he left the bedroll open.

He awoke several times during the night, as he usually did when out on the trail. Twice he slipped out of the bedroll, then walked to the lip of the depression to check the horizon. Once again there was enough of a moon for him to see a considerable distance. No signs of other humans, no gleam of a campfire or smell of smoke. No Crow warriors crawling up on his camp, eager to take hair, or horses, or both. Long Rider was fully aware that a man who relaxed out here on the prairie usually ended up dead. The Indian way was the way of constant minor warfare. He had grown up with that way and was comfortable with it. It kept him alive . . . in more ways than one.

He rode on the next morning, knowing that he was going to have to find water for his horses. It was not a big problem; he was heading generally west. Many rivers lay in that direction.

It was about midday when, much to his embarrassment, he let himself be surprised. He was only partially mollified when he realized that the men who surprised him were just as surprised as himself. By then he was in lightly wooded country. Three horsemen came riding out into a clearing just as Long Rider came out into the open on the clearing's opposite side. All four men pulled their horses up hard. Long Rider's right hand drifted down toward the butt of his Winchester . . . then he saw that the three riders on the opposite side of the little meadow were Cheyenne. Allies. Well . . . usually.

He raised his right hand in a symbol of greeting, of lack of hostile intent. The three Cheyenne did not at first return the gesture. He saw them staring at him, apparently a little perplexed.

It took Long Rider a moment to figure out why they appeared so hesitant. Then he understood . . . it was his Oglala clothing and bearing put against his white man's hair and eyes.

To gain their confidence, he rode toward them slowly, with his hands well away from his weapons. Stopping again, just a few yards away, he took the opportunity to study the three Cheyenne, just as openly as they were studying him. They were quite separate in age: an older man, another man a little older than Long Rider, and a third, considerably younger. All three were quite ragged and looked underfed. He greeted them in Cheyenne.

It was the oldest of the three who answered. "Tell us," he said. "Help us in our confusion. What kind of man are you?"

"I am Lakota," Long Rider replied, just a little stiffly. "Of the Oglala Bad Faces."

The Cheyenne nodded. Dubiously. "You sound like an Oglala, and you bear an Oglala's marks. Yet . . ."

The man was looking again at Long Rider's hair and

eyes, at his skin. "I am called Long Rider," he finally told the Cheyenne.

The man's eyes lit up. "Ah!" he burst out. He turned to the others. "We have met a great warrior. This is the Oglala who made that famous ride through the snow."

The next oldest man smiled at Long Rider, apparently in recognition of, if not the name, then the deed. The younger man, who had a rather sullen look about him, did not react. The older Cheyenne decided to enlighten him. "Many winters ago," he said to the young man, "the soldiers came into this country. In this man's camp, there were only the young and the old; the warriors were out hunting. When it was known that the soldiers' route would take them straight to another camp of Oglala, this man, who at the time had only . . ."

He turned back to face Long Rider. "How many winters did you have?" he asked.

"Fourteen."

The Cheyenne turned back to the youngest man. "Fourteen winters. And he rode through a blizzard for days, killing many horses beneath him. He reached the camp in time, and they were able to move away before the soldiers arrived. That is how he got his name . . . from that long, difficult ride. And with only fourteen winters!"

The Cheyenne was smiling. Long Rider modestly kept a smile from his face, although he was glowing inside at the Cheyenne's recitation of his deed . . . even if it was a little overdone. No man minds having his accomplishments recited in front of others. Certainly few Lakota warriors would mind.

But the young Cheyenne seemed unimpressed. "Nowadays," he grumbled, "what man can hope for such an adventure? The most excitement he is likely to find is to have one of the Indian Agent's tame cows fall on him when he kills it."

Long Rider was struck by the bitterness in the young man's voice, and once again he noticed the ragged, gaunt appearance of all three of them. "What brings you here?" he asked the older man.

The Cheyenne, who now introduced himself as White Cloud, stopped smiling. "We ran away from the reservation," he said sadly. "The people were starving. The Agent had not brought enough beef, and there is not much else to eat. We left, as hungry as you see us, to see if we could find food."

"And perhaps kill some white men," the youngest man snorted, his voice just as bitter as before. Long Rider looked at him more closely. In spite of his bellicose words, there was something about him that looked weak, shifty. The other man, Black Buffalo, sat his horse quietly, not paying much attention to the conversation, just staring vacantly into space, as if whatever he saw inside his own mind was far more interesting than whatever might exist in the outside world.

After they had all watered their horses at a little stream, it was decided, almost wordlessly, that they would ride on together. As they rode, White Cloud asked Long Rider where he was heading. "Away," was Long Rider's only response. White Cloud did not press for more details.

They rode for about an hour. The trees had been left behind, and now they were on the open prairie again. Long Rider saw a glint of white about half a mile away, and for a moment he thought it might be leftover patches of snow. But that could not be, it had not snowed for a long time. Then, as the four men rode closer, they saw that the white glaze on the prairie was caused by piles of bones. Hundreds and hundreds of piles of bones. Buffalo bones. Perhaps the bones of thousands of animals.

It took them half an hour to pass through the boneyard, the wreckage left by hide hunters. Thousands of animals killed, only for their hides, the meat left to rot, food only for scavengers. Finally, White Cloud burst out, "They have taken everything, those white men, those killers without purpose. They have left us nothing. The buffalo are gone. Those vast herds. All gone. And only a few years ago there were more than could ever be counted. And for what? Why were so many killed? Do the white men need to build so many lodges, make so many buffalo robes? Can there be so many of them?"

Long Rider said nothing. He knew that the relentless slaughter of the buffalo by the white hunters had not been for nothing. Nor had it been to provide lodges and robes from their hides, because the white men did not live in lodges. No, it had been done for greed, for profit, for the sale of those thick, fleecy hides, carelessly thrown on living room floors in the White Man's houses, not only in the East, but in Europe. And, worse, the buffalo had been nearly exterminated to rid the range of their vast numbers, so that there would be nothing to compete with the White Man's cattle, when he finally moved them onto these rich grassy plains. But he said none of this to White Cloud. The older man's misery was as complete as it was ever going to get.

The shadows were growing long when they saw trees ahead, and low, rolling terrain. There they would find water. But no food, and Long Rider had already passed out most of his dried meat among the hungry Cheyenne. However, luck intervened. Their horses, smelling water, had just picked up their weary pace, when Long Rider saw movement off to their left.

He stopped his horse. The movement had stopped, too, and now he could make out the form of an antelope, standing motionless on a small rise about four hundred yards away. By now, the others had seen it, too. Their mouths watered. Long Rider saw White Cloud finger his ancient rifle. "Too far away," White Cloud murmured.

All of them knew that there was no point in trying to chase the antelope; it could easily outdistance their burdened, tired horses. The three Cheyenne had already accepted the prospect of another hungry camp, when Long Rider slid from the back of his horse. "Ride on a ways," he told White Cloud.

Long Rider had made, out of skins, a double sling to hold his rifles. The sling hung over his horse's withers, the Winchester on the right, the big single-shot on the left. He now slid the single-shot from its makeshift scabbard. The three Cheyenne were watching him curiously. "Ride a little further," he said again to White Cloud. "Make the antelope think we are all riding away."

However, he did not release his horse to the others; no warrior dared let himself be separated from his horse, unless he was with those he knew he could trust with his life, and he did not know these Cheyenne anywhere near that well. He particularly did not trust the youngest, Badger.

White Cloud shrugged, then led his two companions away. Long Rider moved forward a few paces, then lay down on a slight rise, almost completely hidden in the grass, but still with a view of the antelope, which was still watching them intently.

Four hundred yards. Long Rider raised the rear sight, moved the crossbar up to the four-hundred-yard mark. He pulled back the big side hammer, hearing the satisfying "clunk-click" as it locked into place. He settled down to aim, placing the antelope right at the top of the front sight. Squeeze . . . just a gentle squeeze against the hair-set trigger, while slowing his breathing, finally holding his breath altogether, until the rifle seemed to go off by itself.

The recoil slammed hard against his shoulder. There was a moment's wait as the huge bullet arced through the air. The antelope tensed just before the bullet struck; perhaps it had been alarmed by the big puff of white smoke mushrooming out from the rifle's barrel. Then it was too late; the bullet and the sound of the shot reached the antelope at the same time, the bullet slamming the antelope sideways. One spasmodic leap into the air, and the antelope fell dead, as if it were a puppet and someone had cut the strings holding it up.

There was a great whoop from the Cheyenne. A moment later Black Buffalo and Badger were racing out to where the antelope had fallen.

Long Rider walked over to his packhorse. He reached into the pack for the tin box of cartridges that he kept there. They should have been closer to him, easier to reach. That was one problem with Indian clothing, or the lack of them . . . no pockets. He opened the box and took out one of the waxed paper cartridges. He'd made them himself, just a few days before leaving the village. He felt the cartridge with his fingers, making certain there was a bullet at the front, and that the powder at the rear felt loose and dry.

Holding the cartridge, he worked the lever below the rifle's breech, which caused the heavy breechblock to slide upward, opening the firing chamber. Long Rider slid the cartridge into the chamber, then pulled up on the lever. The breechblock slammed closed, and as it did, its sharp rear end sheared off the end of the paper cartridge, exposing the powder. He flicked away the old exploded percussion cap, then firmly pushed another into place on the nipple. His rifle was now ready to fire again. He had a horror of unloaded guns.

White Cloud had remained sitting his horse a number of yards away, but when the two other Cheyenne came riding back with the dead antelope slung across the withers of Black Buffalo's horse, White Cloud rode over to Long Rider. "Your rifle shoots forever," he said simply.

"Almost forever," Long Rider replied somberly. By now Black Buffalo and Badger were crowding in close. All their attention was riveted on this magic weapon. "It is a Sharps carbine," Long Rider explained, seeing that their eyes were full of questions. "It is the kind of rifle that the white men use to kill so many buffalo."

"Did you kill a white man to get it?" Badger asked excitedly.

"No. But a white man gave it to me. Jim Bridger, the scout."

"Ah!" White Cloud shot back. "Blanket Chief Bridger. A brave man. You are lucky to have his gun."

But now Badger's face had returned to its usual sour look. "It would have been better if you had killed him for it," he muttered.

Long Rider shot the young man a hard look. What Badger had just said bordered on a challenge, a criticism of Long Rider's courage and judgment. However, the expressions on the faces of White Cloud and Black Buffalo asked him to forget it, to consider that Badger was still almost a boy. A foolish boy.

"Come. Let us go and cook some of this meat," Long Rider said. He led the way toward the line of trees ahead, which indicated a stream, a good place for preparing and cooking their kill. The others followed, but Long Rider made sure that he knew where each of them was at every moment, not so much because of overt distrust, but out of ingrained caution.

Within a very short time the antelope had been gutted and a fire started. Half an hour later, choice portions of meat were sizzling over glowing coals. While the meat cooked, Long Rider became aware of the glances Badger kept throwing in the direction of his Sharps. On impulse, he held it out to the young man. "Here," he said. "You try it."

Badger's face lit up. He came up to Long Rider, took the rifle boldly. Long Rider showed him how to adjust the rear sight. The target was a rock about the size of a man, perhaps two hundred yards away. An easy shot with the Sharps, but difficult with any of the other weapons in the camp.

Badger took a long time sighting. He jerked the trigger too hard, but he hit the rock easily. His face beamed. He wanted to shoot again, but Long Rider said he did not have enough cartridges, that those left should be used on meat. "Or enemies," Badger said fiercely. A very warlike youth, Long Rider decided, although the tolerant smiles of the other two Cheyenne, behind Badger's back, suggested that Badger had not yet put his fierceness to the test.

Long Rider ate some of the meat, then went down to the stream to clean the powder residue from the Sharps's firing chamber and barrel. When Bridger had given him the rifle, he'd insisted that Long Rider never let the rifle go uncleaned after being fired. "That there powder's nasty stuff," Bridger had told him. "It'll eat the barrel right out."

Bridger. The man whose name he bore—his White Man's name. Bridger's fellow mountain men called him Old Gabe, after the angel Gabriel, because of Bridger's rather dramatic nature. Long Rider's mother, who had known Jim Bridger for years, called her son Young Gabe, after her friend. Long Rider had resented that for a while, because it was Bridger who'd kidnapped him from his lodge, with his mother's connivance, Bridger who'd taken him to live among the whites. Taken him to a fort full of white soldiers, the old enemy, where, as soon as Bridger had left, Long Rider had ended up spending three miserable years in the guardhouse. Three years locked away from the sun and air and sky. Three . . .

Eating antelope meat, snarling internally over his past, Long Rider once again became aware of the way Badger was looking at him. Or looking at the Sharps. It was a look of sheer acquisitiveness, and now Long Rider began to regret that he'd let the young man fire the gun.

By now it was growing dark. No one seemed eager to sit by the fire and tell stories. The three Cheyenne, with their bellies full of meat for the first time in days, were fighting to keep awake. Each of them drifted a little apart, to find his own place to sleep. Long Rider chose a place with a low ridge of rock to guard his back, and when he finally lay down, and was certain that the others were not watching, he put his revolver inside his bedroll. After carefully checking to see that all the percussion caps were firmly in place.

Still, he did not completely fall asleep, so he was not as startled as White Cloud and Badger when Black Buffalo suddenly let out a terrible cry.

Each of the others was on his feet in an instant, weapon in hand, looking around for whatever it was that had assaulted Black Buffalo. But there was no one, nothing, simply Black Buffalo, sitting up. There was enough firelight for Long Rider to see that Black Buffalo's eyes were open wide, glinting wildly. There was a look of sheer terror on his face.

"What is it?" White Cloud called out.

Black Buffalo continued to stare for another moment. When he finally answered, his voice sounded hollow, as if he were speaking from far away. "A dream," he said. "No. . . . More than a dream. A vision."

Black Buffalo's right arm rose slowly. Still staring, he pointed at their surroundings, the stream below, the rolling, grassy terrain. "Blood," he said. "The water rose from the stream, but it was not water, it was blood. And that blood covered everything in this place where we now lie. It was the blood of men, the blood of horses. And with that blood, I heard the cries of men dying, of men wounded. Everywhere, there was blood, soaking into the ground. And that terrible crying out."

By now, the hair was standing up on the head of every one of those listening to Black Buffalo. Long Rider included. He had grown up with dreams, with visions, they had guided much that he had done. And when White Cloud whispered to him, "Black Buffalo is a man of visions; even the old men listen to him," Long Rider was not surprised. He had already noticed how Black Buffalo seemed to be continuously looking past this world into some other place seen only by him. Long Rider shuddered.

Black Buffalo refused to go back to sleep. Instead, he moved away about a hundred yards, to a low knoll, where he sat cross-legged on his blanket and began to sing and chant in a very low voice. The sound of the chanting sent another chill up Long Rider's spine. He turned toward White Cloud, who had not yet gone back to his own blankets. "I, too, feel something about this place," he said. "Tell me . . . do you know if it has a name?"

White Cloud shrugged. "I have heard it called the Place of the Greasy Grass."

Long Rider thought for a moment. "I have heard that name before. I think that the white men have a different name for it, but I cannot remember what it is."

Badger had come closer. "You know many things about the whites, don't you?" he asked. His voice was not friendly.

Long Rider looked straight at Badger, which, among the Plains Indians, was a very rude thing to do. Normally, a polite man looked down or to the side when he was talking to another man. To look someone directly in the eyes was a form of challenge.

Badger read the challenge, knew he'd gone too far, that he would have to either shut up or fight. He chose to shut up, which did little to gain him Long Rider's respect. Now, they all moved apart again, toward their sleeping places, but Long Rider noticed, before Badger had gone away into the darkness, that he was once again looking hungrily at the Sharps.

Long Rider lay down on top of his bedroll, this time with his pistol lying half beneath his right armpit. He preferred it there, so that he could reach across with his left hand if he needed the pistol. He was not left-handed, but years ago his right index finger had been broken, and had healed badly, so that the first joint pointed away from the other fingers, toward the thumb. It had taken him a long time to learn to shoot as well with his left hand as with his right, but he had learned very well . . . to the regret of many a man who'd challenged him.

He did not go to sleep. Black Buffalo's low chanting from up on the hill lay in the back of his consciousness, just loud enough to mask other sounds, which he did not like. And while he lay there, he flexed his right index finger. The joint was stiff, but had not caused him any pain for years. He remembered the solid smack of his fist hitting against Captain Price's jaw, the sharp pain as his finger broke. With the wound in his palm, he had not been able to close his fist tightly enough.

His thoughts shut off as he became aware of something moving, not far from him. He did not actually hear it, not so that he could pinpoint the sound, nor could he see movement, but he was certain that someone was out there . . . and growing closer.

The boy was good, he had to admit that. He moved without sound, on his belly, worming his way through the grass. He was only a few yards away when Long Rider caught a glimpse of starlight glinting off the blade of a long skinning knife.

He let the boy get very close, so that he thought Long Rider had not heard him. Then Long Rider slid the pistol from beneath his arm, and, aiming over his chest, cocked the hammer . . . almost in Badger's face. "Are you so ready to die?" he asked the boy.

Badger froze in place. He was close enough for Long Rider to make out some of his features. He read a blend of surprise, fear, and hatred. A dangerous combination. But fear of the pistol won out. Slowly, Badger began to crawl backward. He was about fifteen feet away when he sprang to his feet, then walked rapidly back toward his blankets, the skinning knife still gripped in his right hand.

Long Rider got up, began rolling up his bedroll. He was lashing it onto his packhorse when he heard White Cloud's voice. "I do not blame you for leaving us," he said. "This is not a good place. I, too, can feel something bad about it. And the boy . . . he has lost all, his mother, his father, his brothers. He has nothing, no one. Worse, locked on the reservation with the rest of us, he has no way to gain revenge."

No more was said. Long Rider mounted his stallion, then turned the animal's head away from the fire's dying coals. Yes, Badger might have reason to be bitter. But if he rode out into the world and acted with such a suicidal lack of caution, he would not be bitter for long. He would be dead.

It was five minutes later, when Long Rider could no longer see the gleam of the campfire, but thought he could hear Black Buffalo's soft, mournful chanting, that he remembered the White Man's name for the Place of the Greasy Grass.

The Little Bighorn. That's what he'd heard a soldier call it. The Little Bighorn River.

CHAPTER FOUR

Once again he rode all day, heading west and a little south now, pushing the horses, which was unlike him. He had intended to travel slowly, enjoying the journey for itself, like any sensible Lakota.

But something pushed him on, and with each hour he traveled, he began to understand that it was his own mind, the bad feelings it was harboring. That realization caused him to slow his pace a little. One cannot run away from one's own self.

Still, he felt bad. The journey had started well enough, with Two Rivers's gift of herself, down by the stream, in the moonlight. As he remembered the girl, the feel of her, it already seemed as if it had happened a long time ago, in another world. In the world of the People. So long ago.

Since then, he had been plagued by bad feelings: at the place of the bad water, his first trail camp, and worst of all, the scene at the Greasy Grass.

A man between two worlds. The phrase came to him again, with troubling intensity. Was he destined to be lost, forever, between those two worlds?

The question was still on his mind when he made camp for the night, a dry camp, no fire. He awoke before dawn and set out again, much to the displeasure of his horses. They seemed to sense his bad feelings, and it made them act uneasy, threatened.

Late in the morning Long Rider could see mountains in the distance, a mighty wall of mountains, capped with snow. The Shining Mountains, the ones the white men called the Rockies. They dominated the western horizon, so sharply delineated that they seemed unreal, like an overdone artist's rendering. They exerted a powerful attraction on Long Rider's attention. Fortunately, the more he looked at the mountains, the less he was aware of the bad feelings.

The country became more broken, rough. He was just cresting a hill when he saw three men, about two hundred yards away, sitting their horses on another hill.

Long Rider and the three men spent a long ten seconds assessing one another. To Long Rider, the three horsemen appeared to be buffalo hunters—shaggy, dirty men, stained by the blood and grease that came with their job.

In the clear air he could not fail to understand the words when one of the hunters bellowed, "A goddamn redskin, boys! Let's take his hair!"

Yelling, the three buffalo hunters clapped spurs to their horses and rode down off their hill, straight toward Long Rider. Instinctively, he pulled his horse around and headed back the way he had come, towing the packhorse behind him.

His first thought was that he'd be able to lose the hunters in this broken country; his stallion should be able to outrun their lesser mounts. But there was the packhorse to consider. Already, it was lagging behind, pulling against the lead rope, hating the load banging up and down on its back. Long Rider knew that if he wanted to get away, he'd probably have to abandon the packhorse. And everything on it.

Which he did not want to do. A hot tide of anger was already building up inside him. No, it was simply that he was finally paying attention to it. Paying attention to the frustrations of living on the reservation, of seeing his people hunted like animals, without being able to do anything about it. For a fleeting moment he thought of the young Cheyenne warrior, Badger, of his bitterness, and now that bitterness became Long Rider's.

He would not run. He would fight.

His path bent around an outcrop of large rocks. The rocks lay to his right. The buffalo hunters had fallen a little behind; they were about three hundred yards back. Once around the bend, Long Rider was temporarily out of their sight. He immediately turned sharply to the right, riding around behind the boulders. He quickly wound the packhorse's lead rope around the trunk of a stunted tree, then he forced the black stallion in among the boulders, drawing his Winchester from its pouch.

The buffalo hunters were almost up to the boulders; Long Rider could hear the pounding of their horses' hooves. He cocked the Winchester, waiting for just the right moment. If he attacked too soon, he would be right in front of them, they would run him down. If he showed himself too late, even if he got one of them, the others would gallop past, out of range.

The moment came. "Haaiiiiiyaaaa!" he cried out, pounding his heels against the stallion's ribs. The big horse, trained for fighting, did not hesitate. There was no rearing, no prancing, just a sudden bunching of muscles that propelled the stallion out from between two huge boulders, to the right and a little to the front of the buffalo hunters.

From forty yards, he shot one man through the head. By the time he'd levered the action, pumping in another shell, he was among the enemy. The first man was still falling, but the two survivors fired their big single-shot rifles. Long Rider had already flattened himself against his horse's withers. Both shots passed over him, one heavy bullet burning a path across the skin of his back.

He fired again, hitting a second hunter somewhere in the body. The man reeled in the saddle, started to fall. Long Rider tried to bring his rifle around to his right, to fire at the third man, but the hunter was already on him. Swinging his empty rifle, the hunter clubbed at Long Rider, who instinctively held up his Winchester to guard against the blow. The heavier Sharps slammed against his Winchester. Long Rider felt sharp pain in his fingers as the Sharps's barrel nicked the knuckles. He tried to hold onto the Winchester, but it spun from his grip.

The buffalo hunter crowded his horse close to Long Rider's. He was a huge man, with a face almost lost among a mass of matted hair and beard. Bright blue eyes, glittering with battle lust, shone from that tangle of hair. The man let out a hoarse cry as he reached for his pistol.

Long Rider beat him to it; he'd practiced for years and had seldom met a man who was faster with a pistol than he was. The buffalo hunter was to his right. As usual, Long Rider drew with his left, firing across his body. The gun bucked in his hand. He felt the side blast from the cylinder scorch the skin of his naked belly. The bullet hit the hunter low on the right side. The man grunted and doubled up from the shock. But he did not drop his pistol.

Long Rider cocked his pistol again, pulled the trigger. Misfire. He distinctly heard the sharp snap of the cap exploding, but the powder charge did not go off.

The wounded buffalo hunter was slowly raising his pistol, his face twisted with pain and rage. They were now only about two feet apart. Long Rider held down the pistol's trigger with his left index finger, then slammed the heel of his right hand down against the hammer, fanning it four times. One more shot misfired, but the other three slammed into the hunter's body, literally blasting him out of the saddle.

Long Rider rammed the empty pistol back into its holster, then jerked the Sharps from its leather sheath. He forced his horse around the fallen hunter's horse, but when he looked down at the man, Long Rider could see that he was clearly dead, lying flat on his back with his arms flung out to the sides, his eyes open and staring.

Long Rider quickly turned his horse. The other two buffalo hunters were still down. One appeared very dead; the top of his head was blown completely away. Long Rider rode up to the other. At first he appeared dead, too, but then he moved.

Long Rider raised the Sharps, sighting on the fallen man. But he seemed too badly wounded to be a danger. Besides, Long Rider could see no weapons on or near the man, so he dismounted and walked up to him. Still, his approach was cautious.

The fallen man sensed that someone was there. His eyes flickered open, fastened on Long Rider. At first there was only incomprehension. Then, dim awareness, changing to puzzlement. "Why . . . you ain't no Injun a'tall," he murmured weakly.

Long Rider said nothing, stared down at the man. He could see that his bullet had taken him in the abdomen, on the right side. It had probably lodged near his heart. He would not live long.

The wounded man licked his lips. "Guess . . . guess you ain't gonna take my hair, then."

Long Rider spat on the ground. "You would have taken mine."

"But . . . we thought you was an Injun. . . ."

The man's eyes closed. A shudder ran through his body. Long Rider thought he had died, but his eyes opened again. "You . . . won't take my hair," he murmured. Hopefully? A dying declaration? A moment later the man's body shook again. Blood gushed from his mouth, and he died.

Long Rider immediately turned away from the man, checking all around him. There was still no one moving on this little battlefield, except himself. There was no one on the horizon, either. All along, he'd been aware of the possibility that these men were not alone, but part of a larger group. However, no one had come to investigate the sound of the shooting.

He went back to his horse. The big stallion, although shivering a little from the smell of blood, was standing patiently where Long Rider had left him. Long Rider shoved the Sharps back into its pouch, then went over to where the Winchester lay. When he picked it up there seemed to be no damage except for a scar on the wooden forearm. He pulled the lever down, opening the action, catching the bright brass case as it flew into the air. Reversing the rifle, he looked down the barrel. It seemed straight and unmarked. He worked the action a few more times, relieved to see that the cartridges fed easily. Leaning down, he picked up the fallen cartridges and pushed them back into the magazine.

Long Rider looked over at the dead men. Scalping. He'd grown up with it all around him, as his fellow warriors collected trophies of their dead enemies. Sometimes they took scalps from enemies who were still alive. Long Rider remembered the one time he'd taken a scalp. It had happened when he'd been fighting with Red Cloud, against the soldiers. During the height of battle, he'd recognized one of the soldiers. He'd once seen this same man beat a bound and helpless Oglala prisoner with his rifle barrel, old Two Face, the medicine man. Just a short time before the army hanged Two Face.

What Long Rider did to the soldier was an act of rage, of angry memory. First he shot him, wounding him badly. Then, while the soldier was still alive, he'd sliced his scalp away. Then he had taken the trooper's saber and hacked off his arms and his private parts, stuffing the private parts into the soldier's mouth. Fortunately, by then the soldier was dead.

For just a few minutes Long Rider had felt a furious joy, but the joy had faded, replaced by a sick feeling. Something inside him had rebelled against his own cruelty, perhaps something his mind had taken in through his mother's influence. He had never mutilated another enemy, no matter what that enemy might have done to deserve it.

Now, standing among the fallen buffalo hunters, Long Rider found that he felt no bitterness toward them at all. They had fought like warriors chasing a member of an enemy tribe. Which, he supposed wryly, was the truth. Were not the White Man and the Red Man of two distinct tribes, constantly at war? The hunters had fought bravely. What better thing could be said of a man?

Long Rider decided that he would bury the hunters, which was the White Man's way. A way he could not understand, putting a man in a cold, damp hole in the ground, far away from the world of light and air in which he had lived. He much preferred the Lakota way—placing the dead on raised platforms, where the birds and the elements would be able to scatter the body in every direction, uniting it not only with the earth, but also with the air and water.

His decision did not extend to digging too deep a hole. He found a cut-bank a little distance away. Using a shovel he found lashed to the back of one of the white men's horses, he dug out a shallow pit, into which he rolled the bodies. Then he began to throw in the hunters' gear.

He hesitated. Time to do some planning. So far, his appearance had gotten him into nothing but trouble. If he intended to travel in the White Man's world, it would help if he looked at least a little like a white man.

The hunters' horses were cropping grass a little ways off. Long Rider rounded up all three animals. One was wearing a particularly fine saddle. Long Rider had seen a saddle like it before; he'd been told that it came from a place called Mexico.

He took the saddle off the horse and laid it aside, along with the bridle. The other saddles and horse gear he threw into the pit with the bodies. But not before he had saved out two rifle scabbards, two canteens, and a fine pair of saddlebags.

The hunters' personal gear he did not touch, but threw it into the pit along with the horse gear. Then, using the shovel, he collapsed the cut-bank down over the pit, burying the bodies.

It took ten minutes of hard work to convince his stallion to accept the saddle and bridle. True, having started life among the whites, the big black stallion had originally been broken to the saddle, but he had been ridden bareback for a long time. After a lot of bucking and general resistance on the horse's part, Long Rider finally had the saddle and bridle in place. Resigned, the stallion stood morosely while Long Rider strapped on the saddlebags and rifle scabbards.

He began transferring gear from the packhorse to the saddlebags. While he was doing this, he laid aside a pair of trousers and a shirt that he'd been keeping in the pack. His last act was to take off his breechclout and put on the shirt and trousers. He hated putting them on, especially hated the trousers, which tugged at his legs and crotch.

Sighing, he dug for the last item inside the pack. An old slouch hat. It was badly crushed, but, after beating it back into some semblance of its original shape, he crammed it onto his head.

Now, except for the moccasins, he was dressed as a white man. He wondered if he should have taken a pair of boots from the hunters before he buried them. No. The trousers were bad enough. Damned if he'd lock his feet up in heavy boots. The moccasins would have to do.

Now, the horses. He considered taking them with him. After all, he was a warrior, and whoever won a fight was entitled to the spoils. It was a Lakota custom. And what spoils could be of more value to a Lakota warrior than horses?

But Long Rider had been around the White Man long enough to know about brands. To be caught in the white world with these horses might get him hung. Nor did he care to ride in the White Man's world with an Indian pony for a packhorse. So he turned all four animals loose. Now that he had the saddlebags, he did not need the packhorse anymore.

Finally, he stepped up into his new saddle and rode away from his little battleground. He had gone only about half a mile, with the crotch of the trousers chafing a little, when he realized he had not yet reloaded his pistol. Nor cleaned it. Angry at himself, he rode another half mile, toward a stream. Dismounting, beginning to enjoy his hat again, because of the way it shaded his eyes, he dug around in the saddlebags and took out a small leather pouch, which he carried over to the stream. Squatting down, he pulled the pistol from its holster. It was a .44 caliber Army Remington. He preferred it to the shakier Colts because of its solid top strap. Like the Sharps, it had been given to him by Jim Bridger. Its mate rested in a wooden box in the saddlebags.

He pulled back the hammer to half-cock position, then slipped out the pin that held the cylinder in place. Removing the cylinder, he lay it down on a patch of cloth, then opened the little leather pouch, from which he pulled a small metal corkscrew. Twisting the corkscrew into one of the cylinders which had misfired, he felt the steel bite into the soft lead bullet. It was a hard pull, but he extracted the bullet, then shook the powder charge out onto the grass. Then he repeated the process on the second cylinder.

Those misfires disturbed him. Obviously, he had not been taking care of his weapons. He remembered, now, that he had not fired his pistols for some time. The cylinders had remained loaded for far too long. The loads had gone bad.

He went back to the saddlebags and pulled out the flat wooden box. Opening it, he took out his other pistol. He slid it into his holster, took his hand away, then spun around, his hand darting back to the holster.

He'd already noticed several stones on the far bank of the stream, averaging three or four inches across. He fired quickly, bracing his left hand with his right, hitting the stones several times.

He walked back to the stream, then bent down to take two more loaded cylinders out of the little leather pouch. His spares. He fitted one of them into the pistol's frame, but this time when he drew, it was with his right hand. Once again his bullets sent the stones flying. Fitting the last cylinder, he fanned the hammer, as he had done against the buffalo hunter. The shots were not as accurate, but they struck in a man-sized area around the stones.

Squatting by the stream bank, he used a damp cloth to carefully swab out the barrels of both pistols, then the chambers of all four cylinders. Next, he used an oiled cloth to lubricate the metal. Fitting the cylinders into the pistols one by one, he reloaded them carefully, using his powder flask to measure an even load into each chamber. Choosing a bullet, he pressed it finger tight into a chamber, then unhinged the loading lever under the barrel, and pulled it downward, driving forward a rod that shoved the bullet solidly against the powder load. He did this for all twenty-four chambers in the four cylinders. When every cylinder was loaded, he smeared heavy grease over the ends of the chambers, so that the flash from one chamber would not accidentally set off the others.

Finally, he pressed shiny brass percussion caps onto the nipples behind each chamber. Two of the loaded cylinders went into the pistols, the two others went into the little leather pouch. He'd get a jacket later, with pockets for the cylinders.

He put one of the pistols into its wooden box, the other in its holster. He'd loaded all six chambers in each cylinder. Some men, fearing an accident, left the chamber under the hammer empty. Not Long Rider; he preferred the advantage of that extra shot, so, when he lowered the hammer, he settled it in between two cylinders. True, there was still some danger, but he had that extra shot.

He spent another few minutes cleaning the Winchester. It was the 1866 model, called a Yellow Boy, because of its brass receiver. It fired a .44 caliber bullet, from a rimfire brass case. Long Rider didn't think much of the cartridge, it did not have much range or power, but the rifle did hold twenty rounds. He'd heard rumors that the Winchester company was designing a rifle that would fire a much more powerful center-fire cartridge. And Colt was about to release a pistol to the army that also used center-fire metallic cartridges. The moment he got the chance, he'd try them out.

Finally, after making certain that the Winchester's magazine was full, and that there was a cartridge in the chamber, he mounted. Funny thing . . . as he rode away, he discovered that the change of clothing was already beginning to affect a slight change in his personality. He no longer felt as much like Long Rider, but more like Gabe Conrad.

So . . . Gabe Conrad he would be.

CHAPTER FIVE

The Rockies took Gabe's mind away from anything except the journey. Total wilderness, rugged terrain, unbelievable views each time he crested a ridge, all of it stunning to a man who'd grown up on the Plains. Most of all, there was a great silence, a total aloneness. This was a part of the continent that had not, as yet, been changed, been profaned by the White Man's mechanical gadgets. Not yet. But probably someday.

In the higher passes he found snow, still so deep in places that he often had to dismount to help his horse force a path through the drifts. He rode on, wearing the Thunderbird coat over everything else he could get on. And he was still cold. Finally he found himself at the top of the highest pass, on what seemed to be the roof of the world. Mountains stretched away on every side, the higher peaks gleaming white in the sunlight, for, although there was plenty of snow, the late spring sun was warm and bright.

As he descended the western slopes, he began to catch sight of the faded blue of distant plains, far below. Finally, he reached the plains. He hated leaving the mountains, spent one last day camped on the western slope, until wanderlust drove him down. He traveled quickly after that, heading west-southwest. He scanned the horizon as he rode, alert to marauders, whether white or red. It was not necessarily his white man's clothing that would attract Indian attack;

the local tribes were not much friendlier to the Lakota than they were to the whites. All of these western plains seemed to be a world constantly at war.

Further west, he began to come upon white settlements, most of which he skirted. With so many whites around, there would now be less chance of attack by Indians. Finally, mountains loomed ahead, much lower mountains than the ones over which he'd just passed. He rode across a gentle plain between the Uinta and Wasatch ranges. The land was getting very dry. Ahead, he saw a gleam of water, and wondered if he had finally reached the ocean. No, it was far too soon.

A passing wagon freighter told him that the water ahead was the Great Salt Lake. Now the land became even more settled, with many farms and ranches. For a while Gabe rode along with an old man, who was driving a wagonload of trade goods. "Mormons round these here parts," the old man said laconically. "Real stern kind o' people."

The old man told him a little about the Mormons, how they had been driven from their homes somewhere back East because they espoused a different religion than the other inhabitants. And because they allowed a man to marry several women. Which seemed sensible enough to Gabe; among the Lakota there were always more women than men. It would be cruel to leave a woman alone throughout life with no man to hunt for her, to give her children, just because of a religious belief.

The old man told Gabe how the Mormons' leader had been killed, how, with a new leader, they had migrated west, settling by the shores of the Great Salt Lake, where they set up their own society, as if it were an independent country.

As the old man talked, Gabe was amazed, not for the first time, by the seriousness with which the whites took their religion. No, not seriousness. Grimness. Their beliefs were without joy, were a series of brutal negations rather than affirmations. Beliefs for which one would kill other men, simply because their approach to the spirit world was a little different. The old man told Gabe stories of the persecution suffered by these Mormons. Then, when they had their own land, they had persecuted others, luring wagon trains of nonbelievers into traps, then massacring all the men, women, and children, so they could steal their goods. The army had to be called in, to bring the Mormon leaders to account.

Massacre and brutality, Gabe reflected, all in the name of the strange White Man's God. He remembered reading his mother's Bible, about a God who seemed just as greedy, just as jealous, just as full of petty faults as his human followers.

Gabe stopped in one town, where he bought a long linen duster. The weather was now too warm for the buffalo hide coat. He also bought supplies, the White Man's trail food, beans and bacon, and canned fruit. He was beginning to wish he had his packhorse back.

After leaving the old man, Gabe cut more toward the south. The land was now very dry. He rode through a country of incredible beauty; stark, painted buttes, strange rock formations. Once again he watched the horizon carefully; the local tribes were very warlike.

As he drifted further west, the land became true desert. Wasteland stretched ahead, as far as the eye could see. A burning wilderness. Gabe rode out into it, but only for a couple of days. When he saw how his horse was suffering, he headed north again. Two days later, he reached the rail line.

He hesitated. He'd ridden on trains before, when he'd gone back East to search for the army captain who'd killed his mother and his wife. But this was a new line, completed just a few years before. America's first transcontinental railroad. Now, a tenderfoot could leave the East and travel to the West in a week or ten days. In considerable comfort, if he had enough money. A journey which had previously taken months of hardship and danger.

Gabe decided that he would try the train. He rode west for another day, until he reached a station, smack-dab in the middle of some of the most barren land he'd ever seen. When the westbound train puffed into the station a few

hours later, he'd already bought his ticket from the lone
station hand. His horse and horse gear went into the stock
car, but when he mounted the train he took his personal
gear with him . . . including both rifles.

This far west, no one paid much attention to a man
bringing two rifles and a pistol into a passenger car. There
were other armed men inside; the railroad did not discour-
age armed men, in fact, it knew that it could count on their
weapons in case of train robbers or Indian attack.

A family of Easterners, a man and wife and their three
rambunctious children, sat opposite Gabe. The children
were enthralled by the tall man with the long hair hanging
down over his shoulders, wearing moccasins, like an Indian,
who sat silently, facing them, with two rifles propped up
next to the window. They stared at Gabe for hours, giving
up their former obnoxious behavior.

The train sped along, sometimes at more than thirty
miles an hour. Gabe was impressed, not so much by the
mechanical marvel in which he was being carried over the
land, but by the land itself, the desert, which passed by
outside the train windows, mile after mile, hour after hour.
What a huge country this was!

Boredom eventually set in. Despite the fact that he had no
real desire to ride a horse across the desert, the pounding of
iron wheels against iron rails began to pall. The Easterners'
children were growing cranky. Once, Gabe, annoyed, stared
straight into the eyes of the oldest, a boy about eleven. The
boy smirked at first, but, after staring back into Gabe's
rather hostile and very cold eyes, he quieted down like a
mouse mesmerized by a snake.

On the second day, Gabe, leaning out the window as the
train negotiated a curve, saw mountains ahead. Mountains
that reminded him of the Rockies. That evening, when the
train came into a station at the base of the mountains, he
left the train, much to the annoyance of the conductor, who
had to hold up the train until Gabe's horse and gear were
back on the ground.

The Sierras. According to the locals, that's what these
mountains were called, the Sierra Nevada. He recognized

it as a Spanish name; he knew that this land had once belonged to the Spanish. Sierra Nevada. The Snowy Mountains.

He rode away from the station, making camp that night up in the foothills. Once again the peace of the mountains settled over him. But this time he grew depressed. It was the train trip, so easy, so fast. Now, nothing would keep the Eastern hordes from flooding into the West.

The next morning he pushed on, with the trail rising steeply ahead of him. The Sierras were, in some ways, even more rugged than the Rockies, yet they had their own personality, and an unbelievable beauty. He passed waterfalls cascading down sheer rocky heights into beautiful valleys. At the few places where he found human company, he was told that, until the railroad, these mountains had been almost impassable. Many had died trying to cross into California, because that's what lay on the far side . . . the fertile wealth of the Golden Land.

Gabe spent a week crossing the Sierras, sometimes stopping for entire afternoons, just to look at the beauty around him. There were jagged peaks, deep canyons, huge trees, the biggest trees he'd ever seen, some so big around that a dozen or fifteen men, holding hands, would not be able to circumscribe the immense trunks.

Finally, coming down out of the western foothills, he saw a vast valley far below, so wide that its western edges faded away into a blue haze with no discernible horizon line.

The next morning found him on the valley floor. Stopping at a small country store, he was told that the valley ran north and south for hundreds of miles, and was more than a day's ride across. He rode on, a small figure lost in a sea of wheat, which seemed strange to him, because the valley was very dry, almost a desert. Yet enterprising men had built canals to bring water down from the mountains, and wherever water touched this unused soil, crops sprouted in unbelievable lushness.

Gabe rode through one farm for most of a day. He was told by a passerby that this farm was the property of one man, a former German butcher from San Francisco, who had recognized the valley's enormous agricultural potential . . . if water could be brought to it. He now owned most of this vast valley. His land ran for about two hundred miles north to south and fifty miles east to west.

One man. Gabe wondered why one man would want so much land. What did he fear, that made him grab for more and more and more? Did he fear something inside himself, some nameless dread, something so frightening that it could only be kept in check by endless acquisition? Or was he simply another typical white man?

At Sacramento, Gabe came upon a countryside dominated by large rivers. He was told that he could continue on to San Francisco by schooner or steamboat; the trade of this vast inland region regularly reached the sea via great river systems.

He was tempted, but he decided to keep on riding. The weather was warm and dry, the land west of Sacramento less settled. The further west he rode, the wetter the land became, until he found himself riding through vast marshes, where the delta of several rivers spread out to cover the earth. There were hundreds of waterfowl in the various marshes and lagoons, a hunter's paradise. Sometimes, when Gabe found his way blocked by impenetrable swamps, he had to backtrack. Eventually, he was forced to follow the main road, the beaten track that would take him to the coast.

He reached it two leisurely days later. A range of low hills blocked off the western edge of the valley. He left the rivers and rode up into the hills. They were dry hills, covered in scattered chaparral, with occasional stands of pine. The terrain was not difficult, and late in the afternoon he found himself on a hilltop, looking down at a shining body of water. San Francisco Bay. And on the far side of the bay, a marvelous sight, a flourishing city framed by blue water, spreading over several steep hills on a narrow peninsula with the mighty Pacific Ocean barely visible on its north side.

It was a good-sized city, with many thousands of buildings, the larger ones clustered down by the bay. Tall narrow houses climbed up the sides of the hills. One street was particularly noticeable, cutting right through the city from the waterfront, winding uphill, toward two small peaks. The waterfront was crowded with shipping. Perhaps it was only the distance, but to Gabe, who generally loathed cities, San Francisco was the most beautiful he'd yet seen.

He stayed on the hilltop for a long time, studying the scene across the water. The city seemed to shimmer in the gentle sunlight . . . a magic place. As the afternoon ended, looking past the city, he caught a glimpse of the setting sun, cutting a red path across the immensity of the Pacific Ocean.

He made camp that night in a little draw, halfway up the Sausalito Hills. As he lay in his bedroll, ready to fall asleep, remembering his first view of San Francisco, he decided that he would go there. He would visit that grand city across the bay.

CHAPTER SIX

A flat-bottom ferry took Gabe across the bay to San Francisco. His horse protested strenuously, not at all willing to set foot on something that moved and rocked beneath its hooves. The ferryman, an old hand at bribery, produced a sugar lump. The horse, following the hand that held such a wonderful treat, was on the wooden deck before it even knew it.

The ferry slipped away from the dock. Gabe stood next to his horse, holding its bridle tightly, murmuring soothing words. By the time they were halfway across, the big stallion was more interested in its new surroundings than it was frightened. Nevertheless, once the ferry reached the San Francisco waterfront, the horse scrambled ashore with alacrity.

Gabe mounted and rode through the streets. Immediately, he was struck by the diversity of the people: obvious white American city dwellers; mountain men; dark-skinned men in turbans, walking along with women in long, flimsy gowns who had colored spots on their foreheads; and Chinese people, lots of Chinese people, dressed in baggy trousers and soft shoes a little like moccasins, wearing big straw hats that looked like inverted baskets.

Energy. Everywhere. People bustling in every direction, full of an intensity that proclaimed that they were important people, doing important things.

Gabe rode for half an hour. He had always despised the Eastern cities. He did not despise this city; he even started to become somewhat infected by its frantic energy. He had originally planned to spend one day in San Francisco, then ride on after seeing the sights. Now, he began to reconsider. Perhaps it would be a good idea to stay for a day or two.

As he made this decision, he was riding down a street called Montgomery. It was quite a handsome neighborhood. The street was paved with basalt blocks. The crosswalks were of granite. There were elegant gas lamps along the sidewalks. On one side, on the granite sidewalk itself, a big round clock had been placed on top of a sculptured stone column.

At the corner of Sutter, he saw a hotel. The Lick House, the sign said. He hesitated. It looked very fancy, in a quiet, understated way. The few times he'd stayed in cities, he'd usually stopped at small rooming houses. But perhaps here, in San Francisco . . .

Then his eyes strayed further down the street . . . toward a massive building that blocked off the view. Its very size intrigued Gabe. He rode on down the street. As he rounded the corner, he saw three enormous arches ahead, leading into a vast courtyard, through which was passing a throng of carriages, horsemen, and foot traffic.

Gabe rode in through the archway, into the courtyard. Colonnaded archways ran around the sides. He'd seen pictures like this, in some of the books in his grandfather's library. Pictures of buildings in Spain.

Then, watching people going in and out of an entranceway, noticing servants and porters carrying baggage, he realized that this immense building was a hotel.

He sat his horse for half a minute, pondering, then decided. Why not? Why not stay here? He had the money; over the past months he'd hardly spent any.

He tied his horse to a hitching rail. Before going into the hotel, he hesitated. He hated walking away from his rifles. A hostler, as if reading his mind, came over. "I'll watch everything for you, sir."

The hostler was young. Gabe looked into his face, liked what he saw, nodded, gave the boy a quarter, then walked into the hotel.

The lobby was vast. Where, in this huge room, was the desk? He finally spotted it, and as he walked toward the desk he was aware of the speculative gaze of the clerk standing behind it. Gabe knew what the man was thinking . . . does this dusty man, wearing moccasins and an old slouch hat, have the price of a room? Back East he probably would not have gotten this far. But out here, in the West, it was always foolish to judge a man's worth by his clothing. "A room, sir?" the clerk asked as Gabe walked up to the counter.

Gabe nodded. The man looked into his eyes for a long moment, unflinchingly, which Gabe had discovered few men could do. Gabe's Lakota soul simmered at the rudeness, although he knew the clerk meant none. Finally, the clerk made his decision. "With bath, sir?" he added politely.

Gabe nodded. Why not? The rest was easy. A porter was called. The clerk gave the porter a key, then Gabe led the man out to his horse. After ordering the hostler to take the horse to the stables, the porter carried in Gabe's saddlebags and bedroll. Gabe insisted on carrying the rifles himself.

Gabe expected the porter to head for a broad staircase, but instead, he led the way into an alcove, where he carried Gabe's gear into a large metal cage. Seeing Gabe's hesitation, the man said, just a trifle smugly, "This is the lifting room, sir. It will take us upstairs."

As Gabe stepped into the metal box, and felt it sway slightly, he remembered his horse stepping onto the ferry. A uniformed man standing next to some levers rolled a barred gate shut, then pulled on one of the levers. Much to Gabe's horror the whole contraption lurched upward. He felt his stomach sink down toward his feet, but seeing how coolly the porter was taking all this, Gabe managed to keep from grabbing the nearest support.

They got out on the third floor, with Gabe's face showing just a touch of green. He was relieved when they finally reached the massive door that led into his room.

The room was huge, furnished with an overabundance of heavy, stuffed furniture. Paintings hung on the walls. There was a separate bedroom, housing a massive brass bed. Beyond lay another door. The porter put down Gabe's gear next to the bed, then opened this third door. Gabe saw the gleam of porcelain and brass. "The bathroom, sir."

Gabe began wandering around his new lodgings. He noticed that the porter was still there. He seemed to be waiting for something. Of course. A tip. Why not? White men always seemed to be waiting for money. On impulse, Gabe tipped him fifty cents. A broad smile split the man's face. Before, he'd been polite, now he was downright friendly. "If you need any of your clothes cleaned and pressed, sir, we can have 'em back to you in an hour."

He'd noticed Gabe's paucity of gear. And its trail-worn condition. Much to the man's amazement, Gabe began stepping out of his trousers. A couple of minutes later the porter left with an armful of soiled clothing, with Gabe standing in his underwear, watching him go.

Clean clothing necessitated a clean body. It took Gabe a little while to figure out the operation of the faucets inside the big claw-footed ceramic bathtub. He twisted one of them, watching as fresh water roared into the tub. After observing a while, he made the mistake of putting his hand under the water, then jerked it back. The water was getting very hot!

Five minutes later he had a tub of steaming, clean water. Naked, he slipped into the tub, catching his breath at the heat of the water. He settled down, breathing cautiously. Within a minute or so his body had become accustomed to the heat. As he soaked, he felt his muscles, tired from the trail, relaxing. This was almost as good as *inipi*, the Lakota purification lodge. Maybe better. Lying back, a thought came into his mind, a thought he'd never imagined he could harbor. Perhaps the White Man's life was not so bad after all.

Two hours later, Gabe was sitting in one of the huge chairs, wrapped in a towel, when he heard a knock at his door. Instinctively, he reached for his pistol, which was hanging in its holster over a chair. With his hand inches from the pistol's butt, he called out, "Come in."

A woman entered the room, with Gabe's clean clothing draped over one arm. She stopped in her tracks at the sight of a man sitting in a chair wrapped only in a towel. But, she'd seen worse. She laid the clothing down on the bed. Gabe got up, went over to the dresser where he had put his money; he was learning.

"A dollar," the woman said.

He walked up to her, put a silver dollar in her hand. On second thought, he went back to the dresser, picked up a quarter, and added it to the dollar. He was aware of her watching him all the way. He remembered, then, the White Man's aversion to the human body. But the woman did not look offended. He figured her age at about fifty. For one long moment, she looked him up and down, studying his broad chest, his long, powerful legs. "Brings back memories," she said regretfully, before turning and leaving the room.

Gabe immediately dressed. He was very hungry; he hadn't bothered to eat this morning, and it was now afternoon. He pulled on his trousers and shirt and moccasins. He was about to fasten his gun belt around his waist, but hesitated. Perhaps the city was not a place to walk around openly sporting weapons.

Not that he had any intention of going out into the streets unarmed. He went over to his saddlebags. Taking out the flat wooden box, he extracted his other pistol. Digging deeper into the bag, he pulled out a contraption consisting of straps and leather. A shoulder holster, which he had designed himself. When he'd first got the pistols, he'd worn one of them under his coat, simply by hanging a belt and holster over his shoulder. But that was neither comfortable nor convenient. So he'd had this rig built, which held the pistol beneath his right arm, butt down, held in place by a spring clip. In addition, he'd had a knife sheath sewn to the side of the holster.

He took his knife out of its belt sheath and slipped it into the shoulder rig, next to the pistol. When he had put his clean duster on over everything, he stepped over to a mirror. Good. It would take a sharp eye to see that he was armed. Maybe, if he stayed in town long enough, he'd buy a lighter coat for street wear.

After putting a pair of the spare, loaded cylinders into his duster pockets, he picked up his hat and slapped it against his leg. Dust flew. Maybe he would get the hat cleaned, too. But that could wait. A loud growl from his stomach took his mind off his clothing. All that mattered now was finding some food.

In keeping with his new surroundings, Gabe decided he would eat the best food the city had to offer. Stopping by the desk, he asked the clerk for the name of a good restaurant. Perhaps the cleaner state of his clothing encouraged the clerk. "The Poulet d'Or," the clerk replied, mouthing the words with a certain reverence. "The finest French cuisine, sir."

Gabe tried to follow the clerk's directions for finding the Poulet d'Or, but he'd never been good with the squared-off streets and corners of American cities. If the clerk had said to ride to a certain hill, then follow a stream toward the setting sun, it would have been much clearer. Directions were so difficult in a city; you couldn't see enough of the sky to orient yourself.

Gabe wandered around a while before stopping an old-timer to ask further directions. At first the man was confused. "Huh?" he grunted. "Never heard o' no place name o' that." Then, when Gabe said it was supposed to be a French restaurant, the old man grinned. "Oh, you mean the *Poodle Dog*. That's what we all call it, mister. Never could wrap my tongue round them there fancy French words. All o' them frogs talk like they was born with a sore throat."

So Gabe found the Poulet d'Or, and sat down to a genuine French meal, served by a very condescending waiter, whose nose pointed straight up at the ceiling. The food was quite fancy, what little there was of it, and Gabe supposed that it was good enough. For French food. Maybe the French didn't trust their own cooking, or maybe they bought cheap food, because each item was covered in a gooey, overpowering sauce that soon had Gabe's taste buds paralyzed.

He left the Poulet d'Or an hour later, with his stomach churning over indigestible combinations peculiar to France, a country where liver damage was a way of life.

He decided to walk off the meal. For the next four hours he wandered the streets, playing the tourist. An afternoon fog rolled in, making him glad he had worn the duster. Despite the fog, San Francisco had a feeling of space and openness that was unusual for a city. He studied the mix of people on the street, an international blending. Many of them were Chinese, some carrying poles over their shoulders with a big basket balanced at each end. The baskets were filled with goods, with fruit, or little pastries, or toys and utensils, most of which were for sale on the spot.

Eventually, he found himself in an area of narrow streets and overhanging upper floors, where almost everyone was Chinese. He felt a little more comfortable here; the Chinese seldom met his eyes directly. A polite people. Wandering further into this labyrinth, he became aware of a strange smell, an oddly sweet, heavy odor.

It seemed to be emanating from a partially open door. There was a sign over the doorway, written in Chinese characters. Curious, suspecting that this was a public house of some kind, Gabe pushed open the door and stepped inside.

The room he entered was dark. It took a moment for his eyes to become accustomed to the dim light. Then he saw rows of what looked like bunks in a bunkhouse, and on each one of those bunks, a Chinese man lay, either smoking a long pipe, not unlike Gabe's Lakota pipe, or lying on his back, eyes open, staring up at the bottom of the bunk above him, as if lost in a daydream.

The sweet odor was almost overpowering. Gabe felt his head reel a little. Suddenly a Chinese man came running up to him, gabbling something in Chinese. Whatever he was saying, he did not appear friendly. When Gabe did not understand, the man gestured toward the door. Apparently he did not think Gabe was reacting quickly enough. From the folds of his baggy coat, the Chinese man produced an ugly-looking hatchet and began to advance on Gabe.

Gabe slipped his left hand beneath his duster. The pistol seemed to grow from his hand, pointed straight at the Chinese man's face. The man stopped in his tracks. "I'll leave," Gabe said coolly. "But not with you standing behind me with that hatchet."

Perhaps the man understood. He stepped back several paces, still holding the hatchet, but with his eyes locked onto the black hole in the muzzle of Gabe's pistol. Gabe turned and walked out the door, glancing back once to make sure the Chinese man hadn't moved.

He resumed his walking. It was growing dark now, and as he walked, he became aware of a growing hunger. The French food had left him feeling queasy; it had not really satisfied his hunger. As he walked, he passed restaurant after restaurant; he'd never seen so many restaurants in any city. He passed restaurants with food from just about every part of the world, food from Germany, Switzerland, England, India, China, and many places he'd never even heard of. He finally stopped by one sign that read, simply, "Honest California food."

He went inside and immediately the smells made him feel at home. The menu listed venison, elk, rabbit, even grizzly. But he decided to try some items he'd never eaten before. Items taken from the Pacific Ocean. He ate abalone, shrimp, crab, and when he finally left, the hunger for which the Poulet d'Or had done nothing had finally vanished completely.

He wandered back to the hotel. He was sleepy. But, lying down in the big brass bedstead, he found the springs far too soft. He ended up spreading his bedroll out on the carpet. As he lay on his back, listening to the sounds of the city filtering in through the open window, he felt himself fill with curiosity as to what adventures the morning might bring.

CHAPTER SEVEN

When Gabe awoke the next morning, it was with less enthusiasm than he'd anticipated. The view out the window did not help. There were no trees, no prairie, nothing but the side of a building. Already, a din of variegated noises was rising from the street below. No song of birds, no soft sighing of the morning breeze.

He left the hotel at ten o'clock. Business today. He needed more cash. His expenses were draining what little he had. He felt vaguely uneasy.

He had gone only a couple of blocks from the hotel, when he was approached by a bizarre figure, a tall man wearing a ragged uniform, patched up out of lace and shoulder boards, obviously cannibalized from various cast-off military clothing. A pack of equally ragged dogs pranced alongside him. "Your big chance, sir, to ensure your future," the man said to Gabe in a booming voice. "Bonds, your chance to buy bonds, backed by the greatest empire the earth has ever seen."

From a capacious pocket, this figure of bedraggled splendor produced a piece of paper, which he held out. Gabe took the paper. It was quite fancy, professionally printed, with the figure of a goddess standing on one side, complete with helmet, shield, and spear, holding an American flag. On the opposite side was printed a rough likeness of the man standing before him. The paper read,

"The Imperial Government of Norton I." Below that, in ornate script, was a promise to pay the bearer the sum of fifty cents, followed by a lot of words about seven percent interest.

Gabe looked up from the paper, at the man who'd given it to him. "You're Norton," he said.

"Norton the First," the man corrected, his eyes glittering. "Emperor of North America, and Protector of Mexico. Also, at the moment, Treasurer of the Empire. That'll be fifty cents."

Gabe almost handed back the bogus bond. Then, looking into the man's eyes, he thought he saw madness. The Oglala had always had a reverence for madmen, those who could see into the spirit world, so Gabe dug into his pocket and handed the man fifty cents. The Emperor Norton immediately turned around and walked off, clutching the fifty cents. His path led directly toward a nearby saloon.

Mad? Or simply a charlatan? Gabe walked on, moodily perusing his fifty-cent bond. A passing man saw the way he was looking at it. "Norton sell you one?" he asked. Then, suspecting that Gabe was a newcomer to San Francisco, the man chuckled, adding, "A lot of the shopkeepers around here will redeem it for you, treat it like legal tender. Old Norton doesn't overdo it, doesn't try to make a killing, so we humor him."

Gabe nodded, then walked on again, shoving the bond into his pocket. A tolerant place, San Francisco.

A few minutes later he reached the bank he'd been looking for. To his surprise, it was surrounded by a large crowd. Moving around the fringes of the crowd, he asked a man what was happening. "Bank's failing," the man said tersely. "We're trying to get 'em to open their doors, so we can get our money out."

"Failing?" Gabe asked, fingering the letter of credit inside his coat pocket. If he couldn't turn it into cash, he was going to have trouble paying his bill at the hotel.

"Yeah," the man said bitterly. "Mining shares. Those damned Nevada silver mine shares. It's like a disease, everybody speculating, even the banks, going in over their heads. And then, when the shares drop a little . . ."

Gabe left the man standing with the crowd, looking worriedly at the bank's closed doors. Gabe headed quickly toward another bank, where he'd been told by his grandfather that his letter of credit would probably be good also. His grandfather had insisted he take the letter of credit, had insisted on Gabe's being able to draw funds via a Boston bank at any time. Gabe had at first refused, but the old man wouldn't take no for an answer. Gabe was his only heir . . . now that he knew for certain that his daughter was dead.

Gabe remembered the day he'd told the old man. In a Boston park. The meeting of two strangers, with Thomas Reid suspicious of this strange young man with the long hair and sun-bronzed skin who'd insisted on meeting him.

Of course, Thomas Reid had long ago believed his daughter to be dead, after she and her husband had disappeared out on the Western prairie, twenty years earlier. Then, to be told that she'd been alive most of those twenty years, living with the Oglala Sioux, and that this young man was her son, his own grandson . . .

Reid had asked Gabe to live with him in Boston. Gabe had to refuse; how could a man brought up on the prairie live in a city? Then the old man had insisted that he share in his money. Not take it, but share in it, as a kind of advanced inheritance. Gabe had finally agreed; at the time he'd needed the money to track down the man who'd killed his mother and his wife. Since then, he'd drawn on the money now and then, but sparingly, following his own sense of restraint and fitness.

He needed some of that money now. Mostly because of a lack of recent restraint. He found the second bank easily enough and had little trouble withdrawing several hundred dollars. Money had always seemed somewhat unreal to Gabe; he was presently aware of it only as an uncomfortable weight distributed over several pockets. Gold was heavy.

But his stomach was light. The day was slipping away, and he had not yet eaten. Determined to finally stop his wild spending, he remembered overhearing two men talking the day before about the generous free saloon lunches.

There would be no trouble finding a saloon. San Francisco seemed to have as many saloons as restaurants. Gabe picked one that looked like a fairly prosperous place. Once he'd pushed in through the swinging doors, he was faced with lots of polished wood, big mirrors, a vast painting of a nude woman half-falling off the back of a racing stallion, and several big tables bent under an enormous load of food.

Gabe went to the bar. A large bartender with a huge, sweeping handlebar mustache, wearing a spotless white shirt with puffy sleeves and garters, awaited him, his face unreadable.

"A beer," Gabe said tersely, looking politely off to the side. The bartender nodded. Picking up a large beer schooner, he began working the shining brass handle of a beer engine. It's all very pretty, Gabe thought . . . the brass, the amber beer rushing into the glass, the thick white foam, which the bartender kept scraping away, until he finally had a perfect schooner of beer, with about an inch of head.

The beer was plunked down in front of Gabe. "That'll be five cents," the bartender said. Gabe handed him the nickel, then turned and looked toward the tables of food. "Go ahead," the bartender said. "Dig in. Comes with the price of the beer."

Gabe put his glass down on a small round table. Empty-handed, he picked up a plate and began filling it with the free lunch. There was bread, cheeses, cold meat, pickles, fish, other things he couldn't identify. With his plate loaded to the point of instability, he went back to where he'd put his beer and began to eat. The more he ate, the more he regretted his visit to the Poulet d'Or.

He did not touch his beer. It was simply the price of admission. Gabe had grown up watching what alcohol did to his people. He'd seen brave, noble warriors turn into animals, ready to kill their best friend over an imagined insult, ready to sell their wives or daughters for the price of another bottle of cheap trade whiskey. Sickened, Gabe had vowed never to drink, and so far, he'd kept that vow.

After emptying his plate, Gabe wondered if he should go back for more, or if he'd have to buy another beer first.

What the hell, no one seemed to be looking. He went back and reloaded his plate.

He was halfway through this second plate when he became aware of a disturbance nearby. A man and a woman were standing only a few feet from his table. One glance told him that the woman was probably a prostitute. Not that she was particularly hard-looking, or dressed that garishly, but, a woman in a saloon, with that much breast showing . . .

She was quite pretty, very blond, probably no more than nineteen or twenty, with an open, fresh face. Gabe wondered how she'd kept that freshness.

The man was big, perhaps thirty years old, powerfully built, but running to fat. His slurred speech and the beer stains on the front of his shirt indicated the source of the fat. He had one big hand out, pawing the girl's shoulder. Gabe saw that the man was trying to work his hand down toward the girl's rather generous breasts, but she kept turning her body, trying to twist away. "Goddamn it, Nellie," the man snarled. "Hold still."

"Mister," she said, her voice tight, "I don't want you touching me that way."

"Don't call me mister," he snapped. "Jed's the name, an' you damn well know it. 'Sides . . . you get paid to get touched that way."

"Not by you!" the girl shot back. Gabe could see that she was getting angry. She took hold of the man's meaty wrist and tried to pry his fingers away from her shoulder. He laughed. Reaching over with his other hand, he imprisoned her arm, then dipped down into her bosom, pulling the top of her dress low, baring the whole of one very attractive breast. "I told you not to!" she shouted. With her free hand, she raked at Jed's face with her nails. Jed howled, backing away. When he put his hand to his face, his fingers came away with traces of blood. Light scratches marked his dirty skin.

"Why . . . you bitch," he snarled. His right hand came around, striking the girl in the face. She staggered backward, then turned with the obvious intent of getting away from her tormentor. Jed immediately followed. Their path led by Gabe's table. Jed had just grabbed the girl by the shoulder, from the back, when Gabe suddenly stood up, simply seemed to grow out of his chair until he was standing partway between Jed and Nellie.

Jed came to an immediate halt. A pair of cold gray eyes were boring into his own, from almost the same height. "Let the lady go," Gabe said. His voice was quiet, but not at all friendly. "She doesn't seem to want your company."

Jed's first impulse was to drop his hand from Nellie's shoulder . . . there was something about those eyes. . . .

But people were watching. Two cronies of his were seated at a table a few yards away, smirking. To back down in front of them . . .

"Get lost, mister," Jed snarled. "Or you're gonna be hurtin' real bad. This ain't none o' your damn business."

His hand tightened on Nellie's shoulder. The girl flinched in pain. Gabe's reaction was immediate. He had no intention of sparring with this moose; Jed might be running to fat, but he was huge, and the scars on his face indicated a familiarity with fighting. Gabe simply shoved his fingers into Jed's eyes—he was standing quite close—and when Jed let out a yell and bent his head away, Gabe lifted a knee into the man's crotch.

"Aaargghhhh!" Jed moaned, bending forward. Which put his face close to Gabe, low down, within easy reach. Gabe swung his right hand back toward his left shoulder, then, helping with his left hand, he hammered the bottom of his closed fist against Jed's bristly jaw. Crack! Everyone in the room heard Jed's jaw break.

But Jed was still on his feet, still dangerous, so Gabe repeated the blow again, with his left fist this time, hammering it against the other side of Jed's hanging jaw. Blood and teeth flew, and Jed finally went down, landing heavily. He lay flat on his back, with blood bubbling from his mouth and his legs jerking spasmodically.

Gabe immediately turned, facing the table where Jed's cronies sat. They were looking at him in amazement. They'd never seen Jed go down before. Not before any man. They sat silently in their chairs, with their hands spread out flat in front of them, their eyes locked warily on Gabe.

Time to head for other parts. The bartender had both hands beneath the bar. Perhaps he had a shotgun there. Gabe turned to go, but a soft hand on his arm stopped him. He turned back. It was the girl, Nellie. She held his arm gently, looking up at him, her blue eyes soft and warm. "Thanks," she said. "That big lug . . ."

"That's all right."

Gabe turned again to leave, but the girl did not let go of his arm. "Walk me outside. Please. In case any of his friends . . ."

Unable to refuse, particularly after having played the hero, Gabe shrugged, took the girl's arm, and headed for the door. On the way out he looked over at the bartender. The man's hands were in plain view again, but his face was just as unreadable as before.

Nellie was leaning against Gabe in a very pleasant manner; he was quite aware of a subtle mixture of firmness and softness. Of femaleness. Just before they stepped out onto the sidewalk, Nellie worked a scarf around her shoulders, covering cleavage that might have been permissible in a barroom, but was definitely out of place on the street. Looking over at her, Gabe saw a rather presentable young woman.

He stopped. She still held onto his arm. "Well," he said, "I think we're far enough away from the saloon. . . ."

She looked up at him, smiled. "But we don't need to say good-bye. Not yet. I want to thank you for what you did. Really thank you. Give you something back."

Gabe looked at the girl more closely, at the open invitation in her big blue eyes. She was offering him a whore's gift, perhaps the only gift she had to give. He felt a twinge of compassion. "That's not necessary," he replied, just a little stiffly. "That wasn't why I helped you."

Now, to his surprise, he saw hurt in those big blue eyes. "I . . . I guess you figure me for nothing more than a whore," she said, her voice slightly shaky. "I . . . I didn't mean it that way. It's just that . . . yes, I'm a whore, a 'soiled dove,' like those mealymouthed churchwomen put it, those old bats that sell themselves to a husband. They . . ."

Gabe was touched, almost alarmed by the girl's obvious hurt. "I . . . didn't say I wouldn't come with you," he said gently, smiling at her. "Just that it isn't necessary. You don't owe me anything."

Now the girl's features opened up into a radiant smile. "You're nice," she said. "Nice and . . . kind of scary. Come on."

She took him down a side street, then into a narrow alley. Once in the alley, Gabe moved cautiously, scanning every possible place where an assailant might hide. Was this a trap? But they had no trouble reaching the door to Nellie's lodgings. The door was sunk into a wall behind a dry goods store. A very private entrance. No one would be able to see whom Nellie might bring home.

The interior was a pleasant surprise, quite clean, if given over a bit too much to lace and bric-a-brac. There were two rooms—a sitting room and a bedroom. A large bed dominated the bedroom.

Now Nellie became very polite, very social. She asked Gabe if he wanted a drink, and when he said no, she went to the stove and kicked the coals into life, then put on a pot of water for tea.

When the tea was made, they both drank, although Gabe was not too fond of the stuff. It had become clear by then that they had little to talk about. Nellie was a simple girl, who, as he'd noticed in the saloon, had somehow, despite her profession, managed to maintain an air of freshness and youth.

She put down her tea, stood up, and came over to where Gabe was sitting. "Do you want me?" she asked.

Gabe thought he could detect a touch of shyness in the girl's question. He decided to believe it. She was standing right in front of him, with her breasts on the level of his face. The scarf had been discarded. He was looking down some wonderful cleavage. "The question is," he replied gently, "do you want me?"

Nellie grew flustered. "Oh," she burst out in apparent frustration, still with that hint of shyness. "How can I

explain it? I mean . . . to . . . to . . . what it means to me . . .
to be with a man because I just . . . want to. A man who
isn't . . . a customer. A man who . . ."

She grew too flustered to talk. The shy and virginal
whore. By now, Gabe was certain she was telling the truth.
He'd run into this kind of thing before, a prostitute, a woman of easy virtue, who spent her days—and nights—pretending passion with faceless men, with customers, when
her only passion was the money they would give her.
Men she might not even like, to whom she was simply
a convenience, an object.

He stood up, took her by the hand, smiled, and began
to lead her toward the bedroom. His first reward was a
radiant answering smile. His second was when she began
to undress, revealing a lovely body.

The next few minutes were wild, strenuous, an impul-
sive spending of physical need. Nellie made love as if it
was her first time in months. Perhaps it was . . . genuinely
making love. She looked up into Gabe's face, her eyes hot,
pleading.

Afterward, they lay together for a while, side by side, with
Nellie tracing her forefinger in little circles over Gabe's bare
chest. "So many scars," she said in a tone of wonder. Then
she smiled. "Been making love to wildcats?"

"Just five minutes ago," he replied. She giggled, then
became bold, confiding. "I sure am sick of this town," she
said. "I was talking to a . . . to a man the other day. He was
telling me about a place way up north of here. Real far. A
place called Humboldt County. There's not many people
up there, white people, I mean, but, they're almost all men.
Hardly any women. And you know how, well . . . anxious
men get, when there's no women around, and they have
money in their pockets. I've been thinking about going up
there. Maybe after a few months I'd have enough money
to . . ."

Then she grew somber. "But I don't think I could. Go
up there, I mean. It's so . . . far from everything. You can't
hardly get there, except by boat. Nothing but hundreds of
miles of trees and mountains. Great big trees. And men. I'd

probably go crazy in a place like that."

She shuddered. "So far away from everything that's, well . . . civilized."

She suddenly fell silent, realizing that she was muddying waters by referring to her profession. They remained together for another ten minutes, then Gabe became aware that Nellie was showing signs of restlessness. Once, he caught her glancing at a loudly ticking clock on the far side of the room.

A customer. She had an appointment with a customer, someone who was probably due soon. Gabe felt a vague wash of disappointment, but he hid it. He also knew that Nellie would be humiliated if she had to tell him about the other man. So he made the first move, glancing at the clock, telling her he had to be somewhere soon. Relieved, the girl fell back into her happiness. Unaccustomed happiness, Gabe suspected. While he dressed, she flitted around the room, naked, lovely, lively. When he was ready to leave, she pressed herself tightly against him. "Thank you, thank you, thank you," she whispered fervently into his ear, thanking him not so much for rescuing her in the saloon, but for wanting her for herself.

A minute later Gabe was back in the alley, bemused, feeling a little, well, strange. Dissatisfied. He wandered the streets for a while, wondering where this feeling of strangeness came from.

He was pulled out of his thoughts by a lot of shouting ahead. The sound of a large crowd. No, not a crowd, a mob. A lynch mob. Gabe got there just in time to see several Chinese people, both men and women, run from the mob, some of them bloody, as if they'd been beaten. A few men from the mob ran after the Chinese people, but they escaped between some buildings.

Gabe walked closer to the crowd, wondering what had happened. Had they caught some thieves? He noticed that the mob was made up mostly of working-class white men, roughly dressed, although there was an occasional flash of finer clothing. Their faces were all ugly with anger and hatred. "What happened?" he asked a man.

The man turned toward him, his eyes hot. "Dirty Chinese heathens," he snarled. "Steal our jobs. Work for nothin', and steal our jobs. We oughta kill 'em all, run 'em out o' California."

Gabe's first impulse was to smash his fist into the man's face, into his ignorant, ugly face. A man of small abilities, enraged by the Chinese men and women who were willing to work hard and honestly. People whom this sorry little nothing was willing to kill, because they made him look bad.

Gabe abruptly turned and walked away. He walked for several blocks before he once again became aware of his surroundings. He was at the top of a hill. Between buildings he could see the bay. A wonderful view, that huge bay, hemmed in by hills, with the Golden Gate to the left, leading out into the mighty Pacific.

But the view did not lift the bad feeling that now had him by the throat. Two days in San Francisco, and its charm had already faded for him. He'd thought it a tolerant place, but its tolerance was only self-indulgence. Yes, there was tolerance, even encouragement, for a man like Norton I . . . because he was amusing. But no tolerance when the citizens felt their earning power threatened. No tolerance for real diversity. A city of egoists, who were in love with aberration for its own sake, because it gave them a feeling of superiority.

He thought back to Nellie. What a different feeling he had about the girl's gift of herself compared to Two Rivers's gift the night he'd left the village. He did not despise Nellie's gift, any more than he despised the girl herself. But . . . what a difference.

He looked around him again, at the buildings, at the hurrying crowds, at the ground, invisible, hidden, covered over by streets. And he remembered what Nellie had been talking about . . . a land far to the north, isolated, a land of vast forests and mountains. What had she called it?

Humboldt. Humboldt County. A land without a city. A land of few white men. Perhaps he should find out more about Humboldt County.

CHAPTER EIGHT

The entrance to the bay was so narrow that it was difficult to see from very far away. But the captain of the *Coquille* had had to find it many times during the thick fogs that often blanketed this patch of ocean, so today, with the sky clear, it was an easy landfall.

Gabe had shipped out from San Francisco three days earlier. His investigations had told him that the best way to reach the Humboldt area was by sea. It was possible by land, but very difficult. Besides, the novelty of a sea voyage had appealed to Gabe, the man from the landlocked Plains.

Forests and mountains. Nearly three hundred miles of forests and mountains. Once the *Coquille* passed Tomales Bay, north of San Francisco, the land off their starboard beam appeared wild, almost uninhabited, just as Nellie had said.

The *Coquille* was a small, white, steam packet. Fare from San Francisco to Humboldt was four dollars. Once they'd sailed, Gabe had risen at dawn each day to study the land to the east. Not much to see. They had made stops. He remembered Fort Bragg, half-lost under a cloud of smoke and debris from the lumber mills. He was glad when they left that place. Then, more rugged coast off their beam, up past Cape Mendocino, the most westerly place in the United States south of Alaska. The wind had been gale

force as they rounded the Cape. The sailors told Gabe the
wind always blew a gale there.

Further north, the wind abated, but not a whole lot. More
forested mountains to their right, past a narrow coastal
plain. Then the plain began to widen, and now Gabe saw
scattered evidence of human habitation, the checkerboard
of planted fields, even the white gleam of an occasional
house. But few of either. Very few.

Then, the bay, and beyond it, Eureka, the largest town in
Humboldt County. The *Coquille* slipped gingerly through
the bay's narrow entrance, avoiding the shifting sandbar
that had taken many a ship. The water stilled to an almost
glassy calm that was startling after the rough swells of
the northern Pacific. To Gabe's left the bay was broad,
almost circular. And very shallow. The tide was low. He
could see mud flats in the distance, and beyond them, to
the north, a cluster of buildings. "That there's Arcata," a
sailor told him.

An immensely long wharf ran from the main shipping
channel to Arcata, necessary, the sailor explained, since no
ship could cross those mud flats. "They load a lot of lumber
over that way," the sailor told Gabe. "Got a railroad that
runs right out onto the wharf."

Eureka itself lay ahead and to the right, a larger cluster of buildings, situated right at the edge of the bay,
with forest crowding down toward it from the east. Cor-
rection, Gabe thought. The shattered remnants of a forest.

Mountains rose close inland. As at Fort Bragg, the air
was thick with the smoke and debris from lumber mills.
The mountains behind and the sea air always pushing inland
acted like a giant pot, trapping the town's foul air, which
lay over it like a stinking brown lid. An ugly place, Gabe
thought. Inland, there were great bare patches in the forest,
where trees had been cut away. Gabe had an instant image
of those mountains as a giant sleeping dog, attacked by the
mange.

But he was not disappointed. Wherever the White Man
settled, destruction and ugliness naturally followed. What

mattered was the vastness of the forests and mountains that lay inland.

The *Coquille* tied up at a big wooden wharf. Gabe, laden with his gear, supervised the unloading of his horse. The big black stallion was getting to be an old hand at crossing water. It acted up a little, its hooves drumming against the wooden deck, but, seeing solid land ahead, it was easy enough to lead it down the gangway and onto the dock.

There was no point in saddling up; the docks were right at the edge of town, and the town was not that large. He'd heard that the population was only two or three thousand. He hired a man with a pushcart to carry his gear while Gabe led the horse. Gabe studied the town as they walked. He was immediately struck by its busy, bustling air. And by the fact that almost everyone on the street was male. Nellie's dream. Most looked like workingmen, wearing heavy boots. Some of the boots had metal cleats on the soles.

However, there were quite a number of men who looked like plain old hard cases, men wearing guns; they did not look as if they were enamored of any kind of work at all. They studied the streets around them with the quick, suspicious eyes of men who knew they had to guard their backs.

Most of the buildings had false fronts, some of them quite large. Shops, warehouses, and stores abounded, carrying just about everything needed to run the White Man's civilization in this far northern space. How efficient they are, Gabe mused.

He found a hotel, checked in, saw his horse sent off to the livery, and dropped his gear in his room. He quickly washed off some of the salt from the sea trip. Before going back out onto the street, he put on his Thunderbird coat. Although it was high summer, the air was chilly, a fog had come in off the cold ocean.

Gabe realized that he was very hungry. He quickly found a restaurant, crammed with workingmen. The food was not imaginative, but there was plenty of it, workingman's fare, huge slabs of meat, with potatoes, gravy, biscuits, fatback, and beans. Nobody said much inside the restaurant, not to

Gabe or among themselves. They were there to eat, and they ate with great concentration.

Outside again, his belly full, Gabe wandered the streets for a while. He found a Chinatown, much smaller than San Francisco's, but with the same quick-walking men and women wearing their soft cotton clothing, carrying various items in pole-baskets, keeping to themselves, looking fixedly down at the ground as they slipped silently through the muddy streets.

He saw very few Indians. Those he did see appeared to be moving quite gingerly, as if they were afraid. When one party of three young Indian men saw that Gabe was looking at them, they immediately disappeared around a corner.

Gabe's dinner was sitting rather heavily in his stomach. He decided that a cool drink would taste very good. There was no dearth of saloons from which to choose. He walked in through the swinging doors of one of the larger ones. It was quite plain inside, a workingman's place, with a long, scarred wooden bar, a splintered floor partially strewn with filthy sawdust, and a scattering of rickety tables.

When Gabe pushed in through the doors, the place had been noisy, but as he headed for the bar he was aware that a sudden silence had fallen. All eyes seemed to be on him. It wasn't until he stepped up to the bar and took a moment to sweep his eyes over the room that the buzz of conversation started up again, although more muted than before.

Gabe shrugged. The bartender was standing opposite him, waiting. "Name yer poison, mister."

"Sarsaparilla," Gabe replied. "If you haven't got that, root beer will do."

The bartender stared at Gabe, bug-eyed. He almost laughed . . . until he met Gabe's direct, steady stare. A stare that was meant to be challenging. No eye avoidance here. "Uh, yessir," the bartender muttered. "One sarsaparilla, comin' up."

A partial silence had fallen again. Gabe kept his eyes on the dirty, cracked mirror behind the bar. The bartender was on his way back, with a dark bottle. Gabe's mouth began to water. He loved sarsaparilla and root beer. Maybe they didn't balance the bad things the White Man had brought, but they went a long way in that direction.

As he reached for the bottle and lay down his nickel, Gabe was aware that a man, one who'd been sitting at a table with several other men, was walking toward Gabe's part of the bar. Gabe kept looking into the mirror where he could see the man. He raised the bottle to his lips, took a sip, felt sweet wetness fill his mouth. Delicious.

The man was now standing quite close to Gabe. He was a big man, beefy, and very dirty. Gabe could smell him, a rank, unpleasant odor, which almost overpowered the taste of the sarsaparilla. A ragged scar, probably not very old, ran all the way down one side of the man's flat-featured, brutal face. "That's kid stuff, mister," the man said, pointing to the sarsaparilla, his voice full of sneer. "You really like it?"

In answer, Gabe took a heavy swig, tipping the bottle high. Yes . . . delicious.

"How old was you when you stopped sucking your momma's tit?" the man asked. Gabe heard someone snicker. The bar had become very quiet again. Gabe refused to pay any attention.

Which nettled the man. "We all took you for an Injun when you come in," he said. "With that long hair, an' those moccasins, an' that buffler-hide coat. Took you for a dirty redskin."

The man had finally gained Gabe's attention. He turned slowly, looked straight at the man, who was saying, "Course, you could be a breed."

By now the man was looking straight into Gabe's eyes, into a cold, implacable stare. He faltered for a moment, then collected himself. After all, he was backed by a roomful of men just like himself. "Naw," he said. "You ain't no breed. Not with your colorin'."

"What if I had been an Indian?" Gabe asked quietly.

Perhaps it was the quietness of his voice that emboldened the man. "Why hell," he replied, "then I'd a just killed ya. We don't let no dirty Injuns in places meant for white men."

A man's voice piped up from further back in the room. "Yeah, you know how to kill 'em, all right, Tom. . . . 'Cept most o' the ones you kill are squaws."

Tom half turned toward the man who'd spoken. "Well, shit," he replied, chuckling. "Why not? Squaws breed, don't they? You gotta get 'em before they can spawn more o' them red . . ."

While Tom was speaking, Gabe tipped the bottle way back, draining the last of the sarsaparilla. Then, without warning, he swung the bottle backhanded, right into Tom's face. It was a sturdy bottle, it did not break, but Tom's face did. Blood, teeth, and flesh flew. Letting out a strangled cry, Tom reeled backward, arms flailing for balance. Gabe dropped the bottle and took hold of one of Tom's arms, near the wrist. Using the weight of his entire body, he twisted, up and around. Bones broke with loud popping noises, instantly drowned out by Tom's scream of agony.

Gabe let Tom fall; he was already reaching for the pistol at his right hip. It slipped into his hand, and he pointed it down at Tom, but there was no need for it; Tom had passed out from pain and shock.

Gabe moved the pistol around the room. He was in a killing mood. His eyes showed it. There was not a man in the saloon that was unaware of the nearness of death. Now total silence fell. No one moved. Hands were glued to tabletops.

Gabe backed toward the door. Still no one moved. He slipped his pistol back into its holster a moment before he stepped out onto the boardwalk. Now, behind him, he could hear a roar of excited voices. But no one came out into the street after him. He'd pegged the men inside the saloon correctly, he'd seen a roomful of bullies, not a hero among them. Disgusted, he walked away, toward his hotel. Eureka was looking less attractive by the moment.

CHAPTER NINE

Gabe went straight back to his room; he considered it too late in the day to start out for the interior. He was asleep by dark, which, in these high summer latitudes, was nearly ten o'clock.

Dawn was correspondingly early. Gabe had his gear packed onto his horse long before sunup. He was out of town and on the road while Eureka was still waking up.

He headed north, in an arc around the bay. The road skirted the bay itself. The tide was out at the moment, and the bay close to him was made up of mud flats. Seabirds with long stilt-like legs stepped carefully, darting stiletto beaks into the muck, coming up with small wriggling creatures.

To the right of the trail was the forest. Or, what was left of it, mostly stumps, with some new growth further up the slopes. Here and there an enormous tree still stood, usually on difficult terrain that had made it tough for the loggers to reach.

Overhead the sky was a murky, grayish-brown, made up of fog and the tremendous outpouring of smoke and wood particles from the various lumber mills. The air was cool but clammy. Gabe felt it sticking to his skin.

Several miles further along, Gabe reached a small settlement. The neat grid of evenly spaced streets and the little gardens behind each house at first appeared to identify it as a normal white settlement . . . until Gabe caught a glimpse of some of the inhabitants. Indians. But in the White Man's clothing, living in the White Man's houses, scratching the ground in the White Man's way.

Some of the Indians saw him. He sensed the tension running through their bodies. A moment later, when they noticed his Thunderbird coat, his long hair, and the moccasins, they appeared flustered. Two men stood and stared at him for several seconds; their women had already darted back into one of the houses. Then the men turned and went inside, too.

Gabe rode on. Taking his time, he reached Arcata within an hour. The air was a little clearer here; there were fewer mills. The town was much smaller and somewhat neater than Eureka. The people in the streets seemed less hardcase than in the bigger town, although there were a few men wearing holsters who appeared to be of the same kind as Tom, the man Gabe had taken down in the Eureka bar.

As Gabe tied his horse to a hitching rack, he was aware of startled gazes. Probably some of the citizens took him for a half-breed . . . until they got a closer look. Apparently, in these parts, anything even remotely Indian brought on a strong reaction.

He stayed in town only long enough to buy some supplies. At the moment, towns did not interest him. He stowed his new provisions aboard his somewhat overloaded horse, but before mounting, he studied the terrain. Arcata was backed by steep, wooded hills. Further inland, he could see distant mountains. Most of the land near the town had been deforested, but the dark green of the more distant hills suggested thick woods. That was where he would go.

A little further north there was a gap in the mountains, suggesting a valley, a pass. He mounted and headed in that direction. Eventually, he came upon a river. The water was too deep and too swift to ford, so he turned his horse to the right, heading east, riding along the riverbank. Half a mile later he saw a rope stretching across the river. A flat-bottom ferry lay on the far shore. He considered calling the ferryman, then decided to just ride.

Several miles further along, the river widened. The water was low, he'd heard it did not rain here this time of year. Dismounting, he led his horse across the stream, testing for quicksand. He got wet to the waist but was able to keep both rifles dry.

He'd crossed because he could see signs of a town ahead; in this case, the smoke of lumber mills. Most of the smoke seemed to be on the southern side of the river, so he was quite happy to now be on the northern side.

He passed the town a quarter of an hour later, a small sprawl of shacks with an occasional structure of more impressive dimensions. And the usual mills. He saw rail lines running out of the town, heading toward the coast. He'd crossed the rails earlier. In general, the land had been devastated.

Past the town, the trail grew very steep; a pass led up into the mountains. By now Gabe was past the coastal fog. The day was warm, but not overly hot, with a bright sun and a pleasant breeze. The country was heavily forested, with tall, thick trees, in general appearance like giant pines, some with a reddish bark, others with bark that was lighter in color.

He rode for two more hours, stopping once to dismount and eat a can of beans. The ground was clean and coarse, with lots of ferns in among the trees. He mounted again, always heading east. The further he rode, the warmer it became, until he was forced to take off his Thunderbird coat and replace it with the light linen duster.

The trail climbed, until it topped out. From the summit, Gabe looked back the way he'd come. Far away, he could see the coast, a great sea of fog. Some of the fog reached inland, snaking up valleys in sinuous, cottony-white rivers of mist. Mountains rose out of the fog, dark green with forests . . . except where they'd been cut away . . . scabby patches on a blanket of green.

The trail dipped again. Gabe rode down into a deep valley. When he was near the bottom, he saw another, smaller valley branching off to the north. He hesitated. No well-marked trail led into the other valley. Which decided him. The trail he was on would only lead toward more settlements. He turned his horse into the smaller valley.

Thick woods forced him to dismount. He led his horse carefully down a steep hillside until he reached a stream. He mounted again, able to ride along the stream's sandy shore. This stream was much smaller than the river he'd crossed earlier. The stream was bordered by a great forest. Further up the valley Gabe rode right into the forest. The ground was clean, open, easy to ride through. There was nothing to compete with the huge trees that rose all around him, nothing but a few ferns. These were the most enormous trees Gabe had ever seen. Stopping his horse beside one of the trees, he felt dwarfed, like an ant next to a cornstalk. The tree, one of the red-barked ones, dwindled upward, an immensely high cone, reaching toward the sun. The forest canopy was so dense, and so high, that very little sunlight managed to reach the ground.

Gabe continued on, riding slowly through a fantasy forest, through a cool gloom that was not at all gloomy. A cathedral forest. He'd seen pictures of great European churches. This forest was like those cathedrals . . . soaring, triumphant, transcendent.

Another even smaller stream branched off to the right. Gabe decided to follow it. The stream meandered through more of the same kind of forest. The hooves of Gabe's horse struck the ground with muffled thuds, sinking into a bed of tree needles. Then Gabe saw something yellow on the ground. Bright yellow. He dismounted to get a better look. It was a bright yellow cylinder. He reached out to touch it, saw that it moved. Very slowly. It was a slug. A huge bright yellow slug.

Gabe drew back his hand. Many brightly colored creatures were poisonous, their color a warning to predators that trying to eat them would cause a great deal of trouble. Gabe squatted on his heels, watching the slug move slowly away, leaving a trail of slime behind it.

He remounted and pushed on, mesmerized by the quiet of the forest. Gradually it came to him that it was unusually quiet. There was very little sound, almost no bird song, very little rustling in the brush to indicate the presence of small animals, the usual forest life.

He saw a glimmer of greater light ahead. Perhaps a clearing. He guided his horse around a stand of particularly huge trees, heading for the light.

And came upon a scene of terrible devastation. Ahead, for a quarter of a mile, the forest had been logged. Totally logged, every tree destroyed, nothing left but stumps and debris. Charred areas showed where some of the debris had been burned.

A ravaged desert, where the greedy hand of the White Man had come down with terrible force. No selective logging here, no taking only a scattering of mature trees, to leave even a remnant of ancient forest behind. Total greed, total destruction, a rape of the earth, made all the more horrible by the magic beauty of the forest through which Gabe had just passed.

How soon before that forest, too, was destroyed? Knowing the White Man, soon enough. Just as soon as trees easier to reach had been cut down. Perhaps someday all these mighty forests would disappear. The men who were doing the cutting would give it little thought. All that mattered to them was money, jobs. Probably most of them thought that such vast forests would be there to cut forever.

Gabe knew better. He'd ridden trains through the East; he'd seen how little the White Man had left. All that land, from the Atlantic Coast to the edge of the Great Plains, had once been a forest a thousand miles across. How short a time it had taken the Europeans to cut most of it away. And someday this land, this land of mighty mountains and forests would be . . .

Gabe forced the ugly image from his mind, turned his horse, and rode back into the forest, his mind soothed as the silence closed around him again.

He reached the stream and resumed his northerly progress. He had ridden only a little way when he became aware of movement to his right, a rustling in the brush, the flash of something moving very fast. Instinctively he ducked as an arrow whizzed past his head.

There! A half-naked man, an Indian, ducking behind a tree!

A lifetime of training took over. Gabe urged his horse forward, not giving the man time to nock another arrow. The man turned to run. Gabe was on him a moment later. The man turned, tried to fit another arrow onto the bow. Gabe crowded his horse close, pushed his foot against the man's chest, knocking him down. The man's bow flew from his hand. He lay on the ground, the wind knocked out of him. Then he propped himself up on his elbows, looking up at Gabe. For a moment there was fear in his eyes, then resignation, an acceptance of fate. The man began to chant in a low voice. His death song.

Gabe quickly dismounted. The man propped himself up a little higher. The chanting ceased. The man stared intently at Gabe. His muscles tensed. Gabe knew what was going through the man's mind . . . his opponent had not yet drawn the pistol on his hip. There was still a chance to fight back. He could launch himself at the man standing above him and . . .

Then, to the Indian's amazement, Gabe reached out a hand. The Indian froze. Another attack? But the expression on Gabe's face was calm, friendly. The Indian hesitated. Gabe extended his hand a little further, inviting the Indian to take it, so that Gabe could help him to his feet.

The Indian ignored Gabe's hand, then rolled quickly to his feet. He stood about a yard away, eyeing Gabe suspiciously. "Why you no shoot?" he asked. "Why you no kill dirty Indian, like other white men?"

"Perhaps," Gabe said calmly, "I am not what you think I am."

The Indian took a closer look at Gabe, saw the long hair, the moccasins, and more than that, became aware of something in Gabe's manner that did not fit with his idea of the normal white man. "You no kill," the Indian said flatly.

He turned and started to walk away. "Wait!" Gabe called after him. The Indian turned, suspicious. "You forgot your bow," Gabe said.

The Indian walked back. Bending down, never taking his eyes off Gabe, he picked up his bow and a quiver of arrows. When he straightened, he looked Gabe straight in the eyes. "Who are you?" he asked.

"I am called Long Rider," he said. "I am an Oglala, of the Bad Faces."

Seeing incomprehension on the Indian's face, Gabe realized that he had spoken in Oglala. He repeated himself in English. The Indian looked puzzled for a moment, obviously confused by the strange things this white man was saying. "My father and mother were white," Gabe explained. "But I grew up among the *oyate ikse,* the native people."

Now the Indian understood. But there was still little friendliness in his manner. Why should there be? Gabe had studied European history. There was as little love lost between some Indian tribes as there was between the French and the Spanish.

Then the other man's hostility lessened. "I no hear of Oglala. Where they live?"

Gabe pointed toward the east. "Very far. Beyond many mountains."

The Indian relaxed even more. If these Oglala were so far away, they could pose little threat to his own people. Now he became almost friendly. He started to say something, then stumbled over his poor grasp of English. How ironic that they should have to communicate in the White Man's language, Gabe thought. But there were so many Indian languages, hundreds of them, so little comprehension among distant tribes.

"You come," the Indian said, abruptly turning and walking into the forest. Gabe shrugged, mounted, then followed. A few hundred yards further along he had to dismount, to lead his horse through a thicket of alders down by the stream. The Indian walked along as if it was only natural for Gabe to follow him.

Gabe smelled smoke, and the scent of meat. There was a cooking fire not far ahead. He moved up closer behind the Indian, wanting to keep him in sight. If there was a village ahead, it would not be wise to try to enter it on his own.

Not considering the way this man had attacked him in the forest. Apparently, in Humboldt, whites and Indians killed each other on sight.

Abruptly, the forest ended at a line of undergrowth. Beyond was a meadow, and beyond the meadow, a stream. And next to the stream, several structures.

At first Gabe thought he had come upon a white settler's place. There were houses. Then he saw that the houses, although made out of heavy planking, and obviously permanent structures, were quite different from the White Man's houses. There were no windows. He saw smoke escaping from one of the houses through a hole in the roof. No chimney. The walls were very low. The only apparent way into the houses was through a small, rounded crawl hole in one wall.

The people were definitely not white men. There were not many, just a few men, women, and children. The men wore nothing but loincloths, like the man who had attacked Gabe. The women wore apron-like skirts and were naked above the waist. The children wore nothing.

Now the Indians noticed Gabe and the man who'd brought him to their village. There was an immediate cry of alarm, and the women and children started to turn, ready to run, but Gabe's guide held up a hand and shouted something that caused the others to halt their flight. They turned back to face Gabe, their faces tense.

Now the man who had brought Gabe to the village began to walk about, strutting, with his fists planted against his hips, elbows out. He was talking loudly, importantly. Gabe could tell from his manner that he was bragging about something. Perhaps about this giant man with the strange hair and eyes that he'd bested in a fight. The other people began to come nearer, curiosity on their faces.

While his "captor" continued to brag, Gabe glanced around the area. He saw a tall, thin man, probably in his fifties, come out of one of the houses. He was quite noticeable; he was wearing strange headgear, red in color. It rose up above his head in a broad fan. The effect was quite ceremonial.

Now Gabe's man saw the man with the headdress. His voice died away. Suddenly he looked uncomfortable, abashed. The man with the headdress glanced at Gabe, then at the other Indian. He barked a few words; they sounded like either a question or an accusation. Gabe's man shifted his feet nervously, then mumbled a low reply.

The man with the headdress did not appear to be satisfied with the answer. He motioned to some other men. Gabe noticed a few of them moving toward the houses. He could see weapons near the doorways. He tensed. Perhaps he was going to have to shoot his way out.

The man with the headdress—he had to be a chief— walked closer to Gabe. He said something, his expression cold, imperious. Of course, Gabe did not understand. The chief motioned the other man closer, and he immediately rushed over. The chief said something to him. Gabe's man swallowed, then asked Gabe, "He want know what you do here. Why you come."

"Did you tell him who I am?" Gabe asked. "That I am a Lakota?"

The man nodded. "He no understand word. He think you come from white men, to kill us."

Gabe vehemently shook his head. "If I had wanted to kill you, I would have come with many white men. I would not have ridden into your camp alone, as a friend. Tell him just that . . . I am a friend."

The man seemed confused. "I . . . I no understand words. You talk fast. I . . ."

Suddenly the man's eyes lit up. "Wait!" he said. He turned to the chief said something. The chief nodded. The other man darted away, toward one of the smaller houses. He stuck his head in through the tiny round doorway, shouted something, then stepped back. A moment later a woman stepped outside. The man spoke to her rapidly. She glanced in Gabe's direction, then looked down at the ground. She murmured something to the man.

Then the chief called to the girl, his voice harsh. She looked up anxiously, then, with reluctant steps, she moved toward Gabe.

As she grew closer, he realized that she was quite young, perhaps only seventeen or eighteen. And quite lovely to look at. Her face was more round than long, with huge, dark eyes, and velvety brown skin. Her lips were full, soft-looking. Her hair hung down her back in two glossy black braids, escaping from beneath a patterned, woven hat formed in the shape of an inverted basket. She was wearing a skirt like the other women, although hers looked worn and old. A kind of apron lay over the skirt. Above the waist, she wore nothing. Gabe noticed that her breasts were quite beautiful, taut and full, turning upward at the tips, ending in small brown nipples.

She was aware of his eyes on her body. She flushed, looked down. The chief said something to her. She looked up again, then said to Gabe, in clear English, "My name is Spotted Fawn. I will talk to Broken Bow for you. I will turn your words into our words."

CHAPTER TEN

Gabe's features showed just a flicker of surprise. An answering flicker in the girl's eyes indicated she'd noticed. "It would be best if you tell Broken Bow everything he wants to know," she said. "He can grow very angry."

"And he is an important man," Gabe replied.

"Very important."

She turned, leading the way toward the man she'd called Broken Bow, who stood solidly in place, arms crossed, looking icily at Gabe. He began to ask questions, through Spotted Fawn. She translated effortlessly; her English, although formal, seemed quite natural. Gabe suspected that her formal tone reflected this special occasion, rather than her natural manner.

Gabe chose his replies carefully. He spoke of himself as a warrior, a man of the Lakota. They stumbled over his name of Long Rider; he could only give it to them in English. Broken Bow was unsuccessful in pronouncing it. Apparently, the translation was equally clumsy, so they settled on Gabe, a single, simple syllable.

Apparently Broken Bow had heard of the Lakota, but only as a distant rumor. He seemed to relax when Gabe told him how far away they were, how many mountains, plains, deserts, and white towns separated them from Broken Bow's people.

He seemed to accept Gabe's story of having grown up,

a man of white blood, among the Lakota. Many tribes adopted the young of other tribes, sometimes as captives, sometimes with the consent of their parents. In a world as little populated as the Indian world, new blood was valued.

Broken Bow soon began to grow bored. Now his facial expression changed from suspicious to pompous. He said something to Spotted Fawn. She looked alarmed, said something back. Broken Bow barked something at her. She lowered her head, nodded, then turned to face Gabe. "Broken Bow says that you may stay with us, at least for a little while. I am to be your voice. I am to teach you the ways of our people. You will be the responsibility of my uncle and me."

"Uncle?" Gabe asked.

The girl nodded, then pointed to the man who'd brought him in, who was beaming proudly, his chest thrust out. "His name is Salmon," she said. "He is my mother's brother."

They both turned as Broken Bow said something to Salmon, and now Salmon's face fell. Looking at Spotted Fawn, Gabe could see that she looked upset. Broken Bow smiled at Salmon. It was a superior, condescending smile. Broken Bow snapped a few words at Spotted Fawn. She nodded reluctantly, then turned toward Gabe. "Broken Bow told my uncle that we are to take care of you. That first we must feed you. However, I do not know if we have enough. . . ."

Gabe understood that somehow Broken Bow had humiliated Salmon. Looking at Salmon's tattered breechclout, at Spotted Fawn's well-worn skirt, and the smallness of their house, he thought he understood. Salmon was poor. Now he would have the burden of feeding another mouth.

Gabe beckoned Salmon, then walked over to his horse. He had a big sack of supplies hanging over his saddle-bags, the supplies he'd bought in Arcata. He handed the sack to Salmon, who took it gingerly, but when he looked inside and saw the cans, bacon, flour, and part of a ham, a huge smile split his dark features. He immediately handed the sack to Spotted Fawn, who staggered slightly as she took the weight, then Salmon led the way to the little house, chest thrust out again, with Spotted Fawn following along behind. Gabe slung his saddlebags over his shoulder, slid his rifles from their saddle scabbards, and walked after them.

He'd already decided that he would unsaddle his horse later; he might need to light out in a hurry. Hard to tell, this was a strange place. The interplay between Broken Bow and Salmon had confused him. Among the Lakota, poverty was a mark of distinction. The finest hunters, the best warriors, gained status by giving the best fruits of the hunt to the less fortunate. Yet, there had been none of that magnanimity in Broken Bow's manner.

Gabe had to stoop low so that he could slip through the crawl hole into the house. Spotted Fawn had already gone inside. Following her, he saw that the floor was below ground level; the house was really a shallow pit, with the walls and ceiling built over it. Light came in through the smoke hole in the roof, enough light for him to see a few possessions and implements stored near the walls. There was a fire pit in the center, with a pallet of skins and furs not far away. Probably a sleeping place. But the pallet was small, certainly not large enough for both Salmon and Spotted Fawn.

Salmon came bustling in after them. He was eyeing the sack of food. Spotted Fawn immediately began building up a fire from the coals already in the fire pit. Gabe saw that she had little to cook with, just a few baskets and an old tin pan she had gotten somewhere. Yet, within a short time she had a fairly decent meal prepared; beans and ham, plus a strange-tasting, bread-like cake, which she had baked over the coals.

When they sat down to eat, sitting cross-legged near the fire, Gabe asked Spotted Fawn about Broken Bow. "Oh, he is the most important man in our village," she replied. "He is very rich. Did you see his woodpecker-skin headdress? And some of the other things he was wearing? His house is full of many rich things."

Gabe nodded doubtfully. "And, among your people, it's important to be rich?"

She bobbed her head up and down emphatically. Gabe noticed how the motion made her breasts move. "Yes," she said, somewhat wistfully. "To be rich is important. People pay attention to you. Isn't that true everywhere?"

Not quite everywhere, Gabe thought, not with his Lakota, but he said nothing. The girl probably had no knowledge of any people but her own and the whites. And to the whites it certainly was important to be rich.

Spotted Fawn looked off to one side. "We were rich once," she said wistfully. "My family, that is. Then, after the white men killed my mother, and my brothers and sisters . . ."

Gabe caught the sorrow in her voice. He wondered if he should let this subject alone, but he decided he had things to learn. "When did this happen?" he asked.

"Oh, when I was small. There was a big dance near Eureka. Some of our people used to live down there. It was a powwow, on an island. I suppose we were foolish, to have our dance so close to the white men, but many of our people used to work in Eureka. They trusted the white men, were friendly to them."

She looked off to the side again, her face grave. When she resumed speaking, her voice was low, almost too low for Gabe to hear. "It happened on the last night of the danc-ing. Most of the men had already left. There were mostly women and children left on the island. You may have seen it, it's out in the bay, just a little way from the town. A small island, easy to get to from Eureka. Several white men went there in the night, when everyone was asleep. They broke into the tipis. They killed. They killed over fifty of our people, killed the women and children. They killed them with knives, and with hatchets, chopped them to pieces. They killed a few with guns, too. Then other white men, over the next few days, killed our people wherever they found them. They killed more than two hundred people, all over the land."

She was silent before adding, her voice a little stronger, "My mother and my brothers and sisters were there. They were all killed. My mother was raped first, of course. The white men like to rape."

"But you were not there?" Gabe asked.

"Oh, I was. Until the last day. Then my father took me back to our village, ahead of the others. That was how I survived."

"And your father survived, too."

She looked down at the floor. "Only for a while. He was crazy for a few days, after he heard what had happened. He and I, and my mother's brother, that's my uncle, Salmon, were the only ones left out of a big family. The whites had already killed two of my father's brothers, but that was war. That seemed a little different. But . . . to kill the women and children . . . These white men, you know, kill Indians wherever they find them. They shoot them down like animals, men, women, children. . . .

"Anyhow, my father wanted revenge. What man would not want revenge? Many did, and for a while, after all that killing, our men made war on the whites. We took back much of the land. The whites had to leave their farms and ranches, and hide in Eureka and Arcata. Until the army came. The soldiers made war on us, killed many warriors. But they were not like the other whites. They did not like to kill women and children. So, many of us survived. But not my father."

Gabe nodded. "It happened much the same way with my own people, the Lakota. Now, we are forced to live on a reservation. I left. I could not stand it there any longer."

Spotted Fawn looked at him with great curiosity, then she smiled. "It is so hard to realize that you are not really . . . a white man. Hard to realize you can understand what has happened to us. But when you talk about a reservation . . . well, we were finally moved to a reservation. But the white men there, the ones who ruled us, they stole the food we raised and sold it. They rented our pastures to white men, for their own cattle, which we could not eat. And when we starved and killed a cow for food, they shot us. So, to save ourselves, we left the reservation and came here to hide, in this little valley. We used to have a big village near here. Now, all we have is this little place."

Almost as an afterthought, she said, "The people who run the reservation are missionaries. They call themselves Presbyterians. They helped the Agent steal from us, so we do not like their religion."

"Ah," Gabe said, "but the White Man's true religion *is* to steal from the poor."

For the first time, the girl smiled. Sitting this close, even in the dim light, Gabe noticed that she had a tattoo on her chin, two vertical bars. With that smile lighting up her features, Gabe realized once again how lovely she was. "Your English," he said. "Where did you learn to speak the White Man's tongue so well?"

Her smile immediately vanished. "I lived with the whites when I was younger," she said softly. Then, seeing the question on his face, she added, "I was taken. What is the English word? Kidnapped. I was down by the river, with an old woman. Some white men came. They killed the old woman when she tried to stop them from taking me. They were disappointed that I was so young, too young for them to . . . rape. So they took me further south and sold me to a white family. For six years I was their slave, what they call an indentured servant, because they paid those white men a price for me. It is part of the White Man's law. So, you see, I had plenty of time to learn the White Man's language."

"But . . . you're here now."

Her face hardened. "When I was fourteen, the wife went away for a few days. Her husband . . . raped me the first day she was gone. He tried again the second day, but I was ready that time, and I cut him with a knife. I left him there, howling, with his hands pressed over his crotch. I ran away, or they would have killed me. I almost died. I was nearly caught several times, but I finally found my people. I will never again let them take me away to be a slave."

Gabe felt an immediate sense of warmth for the girl. She was no spoiled, weak white woman. She reminded him of an Oglala woman, as ready to fight as any man. She was not soft, but neither was she brittle.

She had more to say; it seemed she had not had a chance to put her feelings into words for a long time. "I came back to nothing," she said softly. "Only my uncle was left. And he had nothing. Everything had been lost during the fighting. And I came back unclean. So I will never have anything, no family, no children. Who would want a woman whose family owns nothing, a woman who was dishonored? Who would pay a good bride price for such a woman?"

She swept her arm around the meager room. "This is the way I will live, this is the way I will die. If some white man does not kill me first."

The meal was finished in silence. Spotted Fawn seemed to have retreated inside herself. Gabe did not try to intrude. Salmon had not understood much of their conversation; he had been very busy stuffing himself. Finally, he turned to Gabe. "We go," he said. "Go my place. Where I live."

"You don't live here?" Gabe asked, surprised.

Spotted Fawn let out a little laugh. "Live here? This is for women and children. Men have their own place."

She seemed amused at Gabe's ignorance. He shrugged. Salmon was motioning for him to go outside. Gabe hesitated, then asked Spotted Fawn, "My things?"

She smiled. "Leave them here. I will take care of them. That is what a woman is for. Even among the whites."

Gabe shrugged. When he left the house, he took only his Winchester, leaving the Sharps and his saddlebags behind. Outside, the light seemed harsh after the dim interior of the windowless house, even though the shadows were growing long. The day was about over.

Salmon led him to a much smaller house. Salmon motioned him inside. Gabe started to slip in through the little oval doorway, then brought his rifle up fast when he saw that there were two men already inside. Was this a trap?

"Wait!" Salmon called out when he saw Gabe's reaction. "Only my friends. I no have brothers anymore to live with. They no have brothers. They live here, we live together, like family. Now you live here, too."

Live here? Gabe looked at the two impassive faces peering at him from deep in this little wooden shack. It smelled. He thought about leaving, riding away into the forest to camp in the open, beneath those immense trees. But, he had never met Indians like this before. He wanted to know more about them. Then . . . there was the girl. He had been struck by her manner, by her mixture of bitterness, ugly memories, courage, and, improbably, flashes of humor. None of the things that had happened to her had, as yet, destroyed her. And she was very lovely to look at. Inside the house, he'd been aware of the sweet smell of her, of how female she was. He would stay for a little while longer.

It took a few minutes before Gabe realized that Salmon's little dwelling was also used as a sweat lodge. He felt a flicker of excitement. *Inipi!* It had been a long time since he'd undergone the *inipi* ritual, a long time since he'd let the heat and the smoke and the steam purify him. A long time since he'd opened himself to the spirits.

He pointed to the central hearth and, picking up a water gourd, pantomimed pouring water over the fire stones. Salmon grinned. "Not now," he said. "Other time, when sun come."

Salmon turned to his friends. The others laughed and joked a little among themselves as Salmon told them, in their own language, how he had come to "capture" Gabe. Salmon's friends nodded eagerly and looked at both Gabe and Salmon with obvious respect. Apparently, this whole thing was gaining Salmon a lot of points. Maybe that was why Broken Bow had been so arrogant to Salmon . . . the petty jealousy of a big frog in a small pond, afraid of being showed up.

Shortly after dark, Salmon and the others lay down to sleep. Gabe made the trip back to Spotted Fawn's house to get his bedroll. As she handed it to him, his arm brushed one of her breasts. It was warm, firm, and wonderfully soft. How much nicer it would be to spend the night with her. She seemed to realize what he was thinking. She blushed a little, but she did not back away, and when Gabe left, it was with the memory of her wonderfully sweet smile.

Gabe awoke early the next morning, up with the dawn. The others soon stirred. There was a brief breakfast of some kind of cooked seeds, stirred into a strong-tasting gruel.

Now Salmon smiled and pointed at the fire pit. "You want big sweat?" he asked.

Gabe nodded. Salmon said something to his cronies. They smiled, and shortly they were outside collecting firewood, while Salmon stoked up the coals. Gabe excused himself and headed back to Spotted Fawn's place. When he ducked his head inside, the house was empty. He picked up his saddlebags and took them outside. When he got back to Salmon's sweat lodge with the bundle, a roaring fire was already heating the stones in the fire pit. Salmon and his friends were shucking off their breechclouts. Gabe took off his own clothes. Now there were four naked men sitting around the fire.

While the stones continued to heat, Gabe took a long, thin bundle, made of deerskin, from his saddlebags. The others were watching him curiously. They nodded approvingly when he produced a pipe. His ceremonial pipe. He held the pipe up for them to see. It was a beautiful pipe, long and slender, and very special to Gabe. It had been given to him many years before, when he'd been in the army jail. It had been the gift of an old Oglala medicine man, Two Face. The old man's death gift . . . the army had hanged him a few minutes later, the result of a small misunderstanding. Two Face, wanting to make peace with the whites, had purchased a captive from the Cheyenne, a white woman named Mrs. Eubanks, with the intention of returning her to her own people as a peace offering. Unfortunately, thinking he would give Mrs. Eubanks a chance to properly thank him for his generous act, in the only way a woman could properly thank a warrior, Two Face had tried to make love to her. She had fought him off, and now he was to be hanged for attempted rape. Misunderstandings like that, Gabe reflected bitterly, between white people and Indians, usually resulted in a dead Indian.

As the soldiers took Two Face and his companion, Black Foot, out to be hanged, Two Face had slipped Gabe his ceremonial pipe. Now, remembering, Gabe ran his hands slowly over the pipe. The bowl had been carved from a special red stone, taken from a quarry in the Lakota's old hunting grounds in western Minnesota. The stone felt warm and smooth against his fingers. The stem was made out of a hollowed-out willow branch. Beneath the bowl hung four strips of colored cloth, along with an eagle feather. The cloth strips were there to remind the smoker of the spirits of the four directions, while the eagle feather, a power object much more potent than cloth could ever be, was there to remind one of *Wakan-tanka,* the Great Spirit, that elusive power that lay behind all that existed. The pipe Gabe held in his hands was a thing of power, the pipe of a man of wisdom.

While the three men watched, Gabe rummaged further into his saddlebag and pulled out a small pouch of Indian tobacco, *chanshasha,* a mixture of wild tobacco and willow bark. He packed the pipe's bowl with the smoking mixture, then looked up. It made him feel good to share the power of his pipe with Salmon and his friends.

The four men sat back a little from the fire. It had burned down by now, to a hot bed of coals. The rocks were beginning to glow with heat. All of the men were sweating copiously. Time to smoke.

Gabe picked up the pipe, with the bowl in his left hand and the stem in his right. He presented the pipe, with slow, solemn gestures, first to the spirits of the four directions, west, north, east, and south, then he held the pipe down toward the earth, and finally, up toward the sky. He saw some questions in the eyes of the other men, but what he was doing, the Lakota way of smoking, apparently had similarities to their own approach. They nodded somberly.

Reaching down into the fire, Gabe scooped up a coal and dropped it into the pipe's bowl before it could burn his fingers. The *chanshasha* began to smoke. Gabe put the pipe to his lips and inhaled, and as the pungent fumes of the smoking mixture filled his lungs, he felt his whole being fill with power, with the power of those strange, ultimately unknowable forces that made up the world. Power to steady his mind, strengthen his body, confirm his resolve. And as he smoked, sitting naked, cross-legged in a sweat lodge with Salmon and his friends, he felt the white world drop away from him.

He passed the pipe to the others. All smoked. When the pipe returned to Gabe, the smoking mixture had been completely consumed. He lay the pipe aside. It was getting too hot to do anything but try to keep breathing.

Salmon picked up a water gourd and sprinkled water on the stones. Immediately a dense cloud of steam arose, filling the interior of the sweat lodge. The steam bit into Gabe's naked flesh. He almost gasped from the pain of it.

Salmon began to sing, a low, monotone chant. The others joined in. Gabe had no trouble following; it was a wordless chant. Sweat was streaming from all four men. The world dropped away from each of them; each felt his inner spirit, his *ni* as the Lakota called it, being stripped of the daily dross it had accumulated.

More water was sprinkled on the stones. Once again steam rose. Gabe could barely breathe, yet he felt light, clean, and at the same time, oddly solid, as if he were rooted in the ground, like one of those mighty trees outside. Immovable. He was now one with everything around him. In a sense, he was home.

The heat began to die down. By unspoken consent the four men crowded toward the doorway, leaving one by one. Gabe, naked as the rest, followed the others as they ran through the village, heading toward the stream. A moment later all four of them plunged into the cooling, cleansing water, where the last of the tension that had been crowding in on Gabe over the past few weeks floated away downstream, with the residue of his sweat.

They dashed back to the sweat lodge, past a few giggling children, who stared at the white parts of Gabe's body where the sun seldom touched. Inside the lodge, Salmon and his friends put their breechclouts on. Gabe looked at the pile of his clothing. His white man's clothing. He pushed it away with his foot, then reached inside his saddlebags and pulled out his own breechclout. It felt good to fasten it in place. When he had, he felt light, unencumbered. He did, however, buckle his gun belt around his waist.

It was still hot inside the men's house. Gabe stepped outside, feeling the air strike his bare chest and back. At that moment, Spotted Fawn, having heard the laughing and shouting, came back from the other side of the village, where she had been cleaning reeds for basket making. The man she saw step out of her uncle's sweat lodge was not the same man she had seen leave her own lodge. Gone were the white man's clothing, the hat, the coat. Now she saw a tall, powerful figure, dressed in a loin cloth, wearing moccasins, with long sandy hair hanging down over his bare shoulders. Even his movements were no longer a white man's movements. They were the movements of a warrior, of one of the people.

Gabe became aware of the girl, saw that she was looking at him intently. And when their eyes met, he felt something coming from inside her, something that reached out to him. Looking back into the girl's beautiful, dark eyes, he decided, again, that he would stay here for a while. Perhaps for a long while.

CHAPTER ELEVEN

Over the next few days, Gabe joined the daily activities of Spotted Fawn's people. That is, as much as he was able. Many of their customs were alien to his Plains rearing. The foods they ate were different: salmon from the streams, seeds they gathered, and acorns, which they cured then pounded into flour. No buffalo here, no antelope, no mounted hunting trips over the vast prairies. After a while, the valley, the thickness of the forest, began to feel confining.

He was able to help both himself and the others one day by mounting his horse, which was growing restless, and riding north, into an area of bald hills, where he surprised and shot a deer. When Gabe returned to the village with the deer slung across his horse, Salmon grinned widely. Instead of being saddled with another mouth to feed, Salmon was discovering that he had acquired a fine provider. Spotted Fawn's uncle had not eaten this well for some time. "These white men," Salmon complained, burping loudly after a venison stew. "They have killed most of the game. They go through a place like a pack of wolverines."

Day after day, Gabe watched the village at work, the women, Spotted Fawn among them, weaving baskets and curing skins, the men working wood and bone into useful objects. He sat on his heels for hours one day, watching Salmon and his two friends building a canoe, not the light birchbark canoe he'd seen further east, but a heavy craft, formed out of a massive section of redwood trunk, a canoe big enough to carry considerable loads or quite a few people. He watched as his sweat lodge mates used fire and stone axes to hollow out the interior of the log then shape its exterior dimensions.

Gabe shared meals with Salmon and Spotted Fawn inside the house where Spotted Fawn lived. She did all the cooking. As they sat by the central fire pit, eating, Gabe felt an increasing frustration that he was never alone with the girl. Except for meals and daily outside activities, the men and women were effectively segregated, thanks to the practice of having men and women live separately. Even married couples lived separately, with the women and children in their own house and the man sleeping with his relatives or friends in a sweat lodge.

That situation changed two weeks after Gabe had first come to the village. One day, after a meal, Spotted Fawn began to pack. "You must gather what you have," she said. "We will leave in the morning."

Gabe did not ask where they were going, but he was surprised. He had begun to consider this village as immovable as a white man's town, and he did not like that. His Lakota, living in their light, movable tipis, literally pulled up stakes several times a year, packed what they had onto horse travois and headed for greener pastures. They had to, once the horses had eaten away the local grass. But these people, with no horses, and in a much more bountiful land, had no need of moving. Perhaps, he thought, that was why they put so much importance on the accumulation of wealth. Not being nomads, like the Lakota, they could afford the encumbrance of useless goods.

Late that afternoon the village performed a ceremonial dance, the White Deer Dance, in which the men, wearing deer hides and deer horns and adorned with most of their portable wealth, lined up and showed off. Broken Bow was the most notable, with his bright red woodpecker-skin headdress and his many metal, shell, and bone ornaments jangling merrily as he shuffled backward and forward.

Salmon, having next to nothing to show off, did not join the dance. When it was over, he went back with Gabe to their sweat lodge, where he and his friends were gathering what they would take with them in the morning. "Is summer," Salmon explained to Gabe. "Time for hunt, fish, leave village. Camp out." He winked at Gabe. "Camp in woods. Is time of year many babies started."

The next morning the entire population, which consisted of only about two dozen people, children included, headed away from the village. By midday they had reached a stream larger than the one they lived on. The country was more open here, but with the omnipresent forest only a couple of hundred yards away. They camped next to the stream. The rest of the afternoon was spent making temporary shelters. Salmon invited Gabe to camp next to himself and Spotted Fawn. Dinner was cooked over open fires. Gabe watched Spotted Fawn, squatting on her heels next to the fire. In this more open setting, with lots of light, away from the heavy slab houses, he decided that he had never seen her looking lovelier.

That night was a restless one for Gabe. He could hear couples moving off into the woods, and later, muffled sounds of lovemaking. Gabe had spread his bedroll not far from the little lean-to Spotted Fawn had made for herself. It was a moonlit night. He could see the soft gleam of her eyes as she lay on her skin pallet; she was clearly not asleep. Just then, a woman's low, ecstatic moan came from a clump of brush less than twenty yards away. Gabe glanced over at Spotted Fawn and saw that she was looking back at him. For several seconds they looked at one another, then Spotted Fawn abruptly turned over, facing away from Gabe. He spent the next hour trying to get to sleep.

In the morning the men, Gabe helping, cut and gathered brush, then carried it to the stream. Broken Bow, backed by his position of material eminence, officiated while the rest of the men used the brush to build a brush dam across the stream, a porous weir that would allow water to pass, but which would trap any salmon trying to get back downstream.

The fish weir was in place by early afternoon. Almost immediately the first salmon began to enmesh themselves. The men waded into the stream and began throwing salmon up onto the bank, to some of the women, who received them with glad cries. Other women took the dying fish back to their temporary camp to be cleaned, dried, and smoked.

While the others were working with the fish, Gabe walked over to Salmon. He'd had enough of standing around. "Let us go hunt deer," he said.

Salmon grinned. He loved hunting. But when Gabe started to pick up his rifle, Salmon shook his head. "Not good," he said. "White men hear shooting. Come and kill us."

Instead, Salmon picked up his bow, then indicated that Gabe should take the bow of one of his lodge mates, who was at the moment busy with the fishing. Gabe shrugged. It had been a long time since he'd hunted with a bow, but he picked it up anyhow, along with a quiver of arrows.

Salmon and Gabe slipped off into the forest. Gabe soon realized that Salmon was a master at forest hunting. He moved with absolute silence, ghosting from tree to tree. Animal tracks were difficult to see, the springy needles that packed the forest floor did not take impressions well, but within ten minutes Salmon was leading them along the trail of a deer.

They caught their first sight of it ten minutes later, a huge buck, with a rack of mighty antlers crowning its beautiful head, standing about fifty yards away, half-concealed behind the bole of an enormous redwood. The buck was stamping its hooves nervously. Apparently it had sensed their presence, but was not sure where they were.

Using almost imperceptible hand movements, Salmon signaled for Gabe to stay where he was. Then he melted away into the forest. Gabe caught sight of him once, or perhaps just a glimpse of his shadow, as Salmon slipped through a patch of fern, circling around toward the buck's far side.

The buck finally scented Salmon, who was by now upwind of the animal. With a snort, the buck started away from Salmon, not yet running, but walking quickly, legs stiff, head up, ready to bolt at the first concrete sighting of an enemy.

The animal's route took it close to where Gabe had been posted by Salmon. It would pass no further away from him than ten or fifteen yards. Gabe already had an arrow nocked to the bowstring. He waited until the buck was exactly opposite him, then quickly raised the bow and drew the string back to his ear. He held for just a second, the muscles tight across his back and shoulders, sighting down the arrow, past its razor-sharp stone tip, toward the buck.

The buck immediately sensed the movement. Its muscles tensed for the leap that would take it out of danger. Gabe saw the mighty haunches bunch, but it was too late for the buck. Gabe released the arrow along with his breath. The bowstring hummed, the arrow flew away, a blurred streak, light glinting against polished wood, then the arrow disappeared into the buck's forequarter, low down, near the heart, buried up to its feathers.

The buck gave a mighty leap, a leap that carried the big animal high into the air and far forward. The buck came down on spring-like legs, started another leap, then collapsed in midair, landing, crumpled, in a dying heap. Gabe ran forward, drawing his knife. The buck tried to stagger to its feet, but it was too weak, blood was gushing from its mouth.

As Gabe cut the buck's throat, he was aware of its huge, soft eyes, staring at him mournfully. He felt a moment's sadness. "You will run no more, my brother," he said softly, as he backed away from the spurting arterial blood.

The deer was thrashing out its final death throes at Gabe's feet when Salmon came trotting over, grinning. "You shoot bow good," he said, nodding happily.

It had been a test, of course, Gabe knew that. A test to see if he could hunt as an Indian hunted, or if he could only hunt with the White Man's weapons. Gabe was flattered. For Salmon to risk having him, an unknown quantity, miss the buck, when the camp needed the meat, was a compliment he would not forget.

He and Salmon immediately gutted the deer. Then, using their knives, they cut a stout branch and tied the buck's feet over it, using hide thongs. Shouldering their burden—it was a very heavy animal—they started off toward camp, leaving behind a pile of steaming offal, which a group of crows had been eyeing impatiently from the top of a nearby tree. As the two hunters walked toward the camp, they could hear the crows quarreling bitterly over their spoils.

A glad cry arose when they brought the deer into camp. As soon as the deer was laid on the ground, the women rushed over with their knives and began cutting it up. Within a remarkably short time, meat was bubbling in stew pots or roasting on sticks over fires.

Spotted Fawn brought Gabe and Salmon wooden platters stacked high with steaming mounds of venison and fish. Gabe insisted she join them, although most of the women were eating by themselves. He made her sit down next to him, then he fed her off his plate, putting the best pieces into her mouth. He could see her flush with a mixture of pleasure and shyness.

Some of the meat juices dripped down onto her breasts, making them shiny with fat. He wanted to reach out, wipe away the grease. She saw where he was looking. She blushed, but he noticed that she was also smiling. Looking past her, he saw a big grin on Salmon's face.

As soon as they had eaten, Gabe started to lie back on the grass. Spotted Fawn looked alarmed. "You are not going to wash your hands?" she asked, obviously amazed.

Gabe had already wiped his hands on the grass. "Why?" he replied.

She looked shocked now. "Everyone washes their hands after they eat venison," she said emphatically. "It's very important!"

Gabe looked up. Yes, many people were going down to the stream. Apparently they had a local belief that eating venison called for special behavior. Spotted Fawn was already on her feet, and Salmon was walking away with the others. Gabe got up. Spotted Fawn had waited for him.

Together they walked toward the stream. Kneeling side by side on its mossy bank, they bent down to trail their hands in the water.

They were very close together. "Here," Gabe said softly to Spotted Fawn. He scooped up a little water in his right hand, then leaned closer to the girl and began to wash her breasts.

"Oh! It's cold!" the girl gasped. But, if the water was really that cold, why was she not pulling away? Why was her face so flushed, as Gabe slowly stroked his hand over first one breast, then the other? Why were her eyes glittering so brightly?

They both stood up together, then, without any spoken agreement, they walked away into the forest, side by side. The moment the trees enveloped them, hiding them from view of the others, Gabe took Spotted Fawn's hand. He noticed how small her hand was, how incredibly hot it felt inside his own much larger grip.

They walked for a quarter of an hour, deep into the forest, until the sounds of the camp were very faint. Finally, they came upon a little hollow, hidden away inside a ring of enormous tree trunks, so private a place that Gabe almost passed by without seeing it. Still holding Spotted Fawn's hand, he drew her into the hollow, then turned her around to face him.

He could feel her hand trembling in his. As she looked up at him, her eyes were huge. He took hold of her other hand and drew her against him. Her breasts were soft and warm against his lower chest. He let her back away a step. She looked up at him again, her eyes two huge, dark pools. "I'm afraid," she said softly.

He remembered, then, that she had been raped when she was still quite young. "It will not be the way it was before," he replied, his voice steady, reassuring. She was shaking all over now, but she was not backing away any further. Perhaps it was not fear that was making her tremble.

He reached around behind Spotted Fawn, unfastening her skirt. It fell to the ground, leaving her completely naked, a medium-sized young woman with a strong, sweetly rounded body. Gabe stripped off his breechclout, then pressed himself against her again.

He eased Spotted Fawn down onto the soft grassy floor of the little hollow. As they lay side by side, he began stroking her gently, patiently . . . her breasts, her belly, her thighs. He could hear her breathing quicken. If there was fear, it was accompanied by a great deal of excited eagerness.

They made passionate love there on the grass. Afterwards, propping himself up on stiffened arms, Gabe looked down at Spotted Fawn. To his alarm, he saw tears on her cheeks. "Did I hurt you?" he asked, alarmed.

She shook her head vehemently. "No! I . . . that other time, the man who owned me . . . I . . ."

Then the words came out in a rush. "I always knew it could be this way. Could be this wonderful. But I was afraid that it would not. . . . Oh, Gabe! You have made me very happy!"

Looking down into the girl's lovely, flushed features, Gabe felt a moment's triumph. Then, almost immediately, he began to experience a feeling of unease. Yes, he had made her happy. But at the same time, he had bound himself to Spotted Fawn. They had bound themselves to one another. And did he want that?

Too late now.

CHAPTER TWELVE

The tribe spent another two weeks by the river, camping out. Now Gabe knew what Salmon had meant when he'd said that day in the sweat lodge that many babies were started this time of year. After months of sleeping apart, the men and women were making up for lost time. Spotted Fawn included. For her, making love, really making love, was a completely new thing, and like many young women, she threw herself into it eagerly.

Exhaustively. By the end of the second week, Gabe was beginning to wonder if he would ever again get any sleep. He was wondering, too, what was expected of him. Salmon, and others, were sending looks his way. Looks which asked questions. Gabe didn't know what answers to give to those questions, because he was not quite sure what the questions were.

Probably something to do with marriage. Spotted Fawn's people did not seem to be promiscuous, except for perhaps this brief camping idyll in the forest. Gabe reflected back on his days among the Oglala, when young men and women engaged in a certain amount of sexual experimentation before settling down. The Oglala seemed to be much freer in everything they did. Gabe discovered himself wishing he were back with them, back with his own people.

Then he remembered that they were now cooped up on a reservation, unable to hunt, to fight, to travel. There was only a travesty of hunting left to them. Each time the Indian Agent brought them some scrawny treaty cattle, too few and too seldom, the Lakota men tried to get the torpid animals to run, so they could hunt them down and kill them from horseback, the way a man was meant to do.

Then there was the alcohol, forbidden by the White Man's law on the reservations, but showing up anyhow, brought in by crooked traders, eager to profit from someone else's misery. With nothing else to do, far too many brave warriors were turning into pathetic drunks. No. Living with the Oglala was not at all what it had once been.

Not that it was all that great here, despite the tribe's relative freedom from white control. There was one factor that particularly bothered Gabe. Spotted Fawn herself. Their hours, their nights, their afternoons of lovemaking had begun to cement a bond. The girl now meant a great deal to him. He smelled the sweetness of her body even when she was not with him, found himself thinking of those huge eyes, remembering how, each time they went into the forest to make love, those eyes would fill with passion.

The truth was, he did not want to leave her. But, when the tribe finally returned to their village, the predictability of daily life began to wear on Gabe. The beautiful forest that surrounded them started to feel like a prison, hemming Gabe in. He couldn't *see!* Trees, mountains, the valley's depth . . . all of it cut off his view. Much different from gazing out over miles of open prairie.

Movement. He needed movement. He had to get out of this valley, ride somewhere. Spotted Fawn was aware of his restlessness. As close as they had become, he could not hide it from her. He saw a sadness steal over the girl, a dread that cried out, "You will leave soon. You will not be with me anymore."

Now Gabe began to grow short-tempered, caught between guilt and restlessness. Yes, he wanted to leave. He found an excuse one evening, while speaking with Salmon and his lodgemates, with Spotted Fawn seated among them, helping bridge the linguistic gap. Gabe was quickly picking up local words, but communication was still difficult.

The conversation drifted toward the reservation where this small group had once lived. Gabe had mentioned how, from what he had seen, the White Man begrudged the Indian nothing but the poorest land.

"Oh, that is not so with us," Spotted Fawn replied. "Our reservation is in a beautiful valley. Many white men are angry that we have such fine land. Some of them had farms there, but the government made them move out."

"Yet, you came here," Gabe said.

Spotted Fawn nodded sadly. "We had no choice. The most beautiful land is no good to a people if they will only starve there."

"It has no resources, then?"

Spotted Fawn shook her head emphatically. "It's a rich land, with its own streams and rivers, and much food. We were grateful to be there. We worked hard, growing food, hunting, fishing."

Salmon had been following the conversation as best he could. "Damned Agent," he growled.

"Yes," Spotted Fawn agreed sadly. "The Agent, the man the government put there. He stole from us. He took the food we raised and sold it to white men. And he kept the money for himself. He rents our land to other white men, to run their cattle. There is little left for us. A great many white men are permitted to wander through the reservation as if it is their own, raping the women, attacking their brothers and fathers when they try to protect them. And all the while, the white men of God, the Presbyterians, sit and watch and say nothing. Their God must be very cruel; He must have no feeling at all for people who suffer."

As Spotted Fawn spoke, Gabe was aware of a feeling of slow rage building inside himself. This local Agent sounded very much like the Indian Agents in Lakota and Cheyenne lands. Thieves, mirroring the corruption of the government in Washington, a government run by businessmen, intent only on profit, on growing richer, greedy men using their wealth to buy and corrupt the Republican party, the party of Abraham Lincoln, for whom Gabe had a great deal of respect. A party that had become a nest of well-fed bandits.

He abruptly stood up. He had made up his mind, and as he did so, his restlessness fell away. Action was at hand. "I will ride to the reservation," he said. "I want to see this for myself."

When Salmon understood what he intended to do, he grunted in agreement. Not Spotted Fawn. Her eyes filled with fear. "You must not go," she insisted. "It is a very dangerous place."

"Hah!" Salmon replied, grinning. "Gabe very dangerous man."

Spotted Fawn bowed her head and said no more. Gabe knew what she was thinking. That he would leave and would not come back, one way or another. But she was too proud to put her feelings into words, and for this, Gabe felt renewed respect for the girl. She had courage. To a Lakota, nothing was more important than courage, nothing more despicable than cowardice or whining. I will come back, he promised himself, promised for Spotted Fawn. Even if it is only to say good-bye.

The next morning Gabe was awake before first light. How strange his white man's clothing felt as he put them on, heavy, clumsy. But he did not want to ride into the reservation as an Indian.

When he went outside to saddle his horse, he saw a figure standing next to the animal, stroking its neck and speaking to it softly. He started forward; the big stallion was mean as a snake. It bit.

Then, in the dim early morning light, he saw that the person next to his horse was Spotted Fawn, and he relaxed. The stallion had taken to her immediately and seemed to love her company. Gabe walked over, smiled at Spotted Fawn, reached out to gently stroke her cheek. "You are up early," he said, smiling.

"I would not want you to ride away . . . without someone to wish you luck," she replied. Her manner was quiet, almost neutral.

"I'm very happy that you are here," Gabe said, stroking the girl's hair.

Spotted Fawn's face lit up into a lovely smile. Gabe felt as if he'd just watched the sun rise. "Will you do something for me?" he asked.

She nodded, without waiting to ask what it was.

"Would you let me put some of my things in your lodge? So that they will be safe."

She nodded again. "Everything you have is safe with me," she said gravely.

Gabe finished saddling his horse. Then he went back to the sweat lodge and picked up his gear. Going back outside, he strapped his saddlebags and his rifle scabbards into place, then slipped both rifles firmly home. He handed his Thunderbird coat to Spotted Fawn. "It's too warm to wear," he said.

The girl took the coat, held it close to her body. She knew how much it meant to Gabe, knew for sure now that he'd come back. And when he handed her the deerskin pouch that contained Two Face's ceremonial pipe, she took it reverently.

He walked with her, back to her lodge, watched her carefully place his possessions on a shelf next to the wall. When she'd finished, she turned and looked steadily at him. "They will be here when you return," she said gravely. "As I will be."

Once again he gently touched her cheek, then turned and walked out of the lodge. He did not look back until he'd mounted and was already riding away. He saw her one last time, standing in the doorway of her lodge, straight, solemn. Neither of them waved as he vanished into the tree line.

The stallion, after weeks of an easy life, was eager to go. Gabe had to rein it in as they climbed out of the valley. Finally! Moving again!

The reservation lay another ten miles to the east. It was not easy going; the land was rugged, steep, and heavily forested. The further inland Gabe rode, the warmer it became. He was wearing his linen duster to conceal his shoulder holster, but eventually the heat became so intense that he took it off and lashed it into place over his bedroll. He took off the shoulder holster and thrust his second pistol into his belt. The knife went into a belt sheath toward his back.

He branched off from the trail two miles short of the reservation. He did not want to ride into it through the main entrance. Salmon and Spotted Fawn had told him of a smaller trail that looped around to the north. Using this trail, he would be able to ride into the back of the reservation without passing the Agency buildings.

The smaller trail was even harder going. Near the top he had to dismount and lead his horse, which was no longer quite so frisky. Finally, starting down a steep, wooded slope, Gabe saw the reservation below him. Spotted Fawn had been right; it was a beautiful valley, a vision of Eden, stretching away for several miles, a much larger version of the valley where he'd found Spotted Fawn and her people.

The valley was a mixture of woodland and meadow, with a river running down its center. Gabe was able to mount again halfway down the slope. He rode out into the valley, into a warm, green paradise. No wonder the white men who'd been dispossessed of their farms had been unwilling to leave.

Almost immediately, Gabe began to notice cattle. Riding closer, he saw that they bore brands. Probably not Indian cattle, then. He rode closer to one small herd.

"Hey!" he heard a voice call out. Looking up, Gabe saw a cowboy galloping toward him. The cowboy pulled his horse up in a shower of dirt a few feet away. He was a white man, young, with a narrow face and slit eyes sunk so deeply that Gabe could not determine their color. "What are you doin' here?" the cowboy demanded.

"Riding," Gabe replied laconically.

By now the cowboy had had a chance to take a closer look at Gabe. He'd noticed the two pistols, the two rifles, the big knife in its belt sheath, and most of all, the way this stranger sat his horse, the way he looked straight back at him, his eyes expressionless, cold. The cowboy felt a sudden shiver pass up his spine. "I'm responsible for these here cows," he said, somewhat defensively. "Gotta watch out that nobody hassles 'em. The Injuns round here, they'd steal the hooves right off of a buffalo."

"You don't say," Gabe replied, his voice expressionless. "I'd heard that this was an Indian reservation. Strange to see a white cowboy working Indian cattle."

"Well hell!" the cowboy exploded. "These ain't no Injun cows. I wouldn't work for no Injuns if'n you paid me all the money in the world. These here are Mr. Abrams's cows. Mr. Benjamin Abrams."

"And I take it that Mr. Abrams isn't an Indian."

"Hell no, mister. Why . . . he'd skin ya if he ever heard ya say something like that."

Although as the cowboy thought about it, he doubted if there were many men who'd be able to get this stranger to hold still long enough to skin him. Even a man as tough as old man Abrams.

"What are a white man's cattle doing on Indian land?" Gabe asked, his voice betraying an edge of sharpness.

"Why . . . Mr. Abrams leases this here land. Been running his cows here for two years."

"Leases it? From the Indians?"

The cowboy spat over to one side. This was getting tiresome. "Hell no. He leases it from the Agent, from Mr. Broaddus. Mr. Abrams don't have no truck with Injuns."

"I see." Gabe nodded curtly. Pulling his horse's head around, he rode away.

The cowboy watched him go. "Jesus," he muttered. "Who the hell is he?"

Gabe rode on, toward the valley's broad opening. He passed some log houses. Indians, dressed the same as Spotted Fawn's people, were moving among the houses. When they saw him, they froze, as if in fear. They did not relax until it was clear that Gabe would ride on past.

Gabe had noticed that these people did not look in good condition. The adults were thin, emaciated. The children had bellies bloated by hunger. His anger began to rise again. Apparently, Spotted Fawn and Salmon had not been exaggerating. Things were very bad here.

He saw more buildings a quarter of a mile ahead. White Man's buildings. The biggest one looked like a fort, with several smaller buildings scattered around it. As yet, he had seen no white men since the cowboy. Now he did, two men, on foot, about halfway between Gabe and the fort. They were not alone. An Indian girl, not unlike Spotted Fawn, except for her thinness, was walking away from the two men. She was walking very fast, almost running.

"Hey, come back here, you Indian bitch!" one of the white men called out. "I was talkin' to you."

The girl now began to run. The men ran after her. One bent down, picked up a heavy stick about three feet long, and threw it after the girl. It struck her at calf level. She stumbled, then fell heavily. She started to get up again, obviously desperate to get away, but now the white men had caught up to her. One reached down, grabbed her by the hair, pulled her to her feet. "Goddamn you," the man snarled. "I said you was gonna do it for me."

The girl was struggling to get away but had little chance against the two men. One of them tore her skirt half from her body; like Spotted Fawn, she wore nothing above the waist. She grabbed at her skirt, and with her hands now busy, the man tripped her, pushing her to the ground. The other man was on her in an instant, pinning her arms above her head. The girl struggled, her legs kicking wildly, but she was unable to break away. The skirt had been completely torn away now; she was naked. The other man was fumbling with his belt. A moment later his pants fell to the ground, showing hairy white legs. He took a step toward the struggling girl.

With all of their attention focused on the girl, neither of the men heard Gabe riding toward them. They showed no concern at all about being seen, even though they were about to rape a girl in easy sight of the fort. The man with his pants down, hobbling slowly because his trousers were still bunched around his ankles, was not aware of any danger until Gabe had almost reached them. "Hey!" he shouted, his face twisting in surprise as he turned, staring up at the horse and rider thundering down upon him.

Gabe had drawn his Winchester from its scabbard. He made no attempt to shoot the man, not yet, but swung the rifle instead, smashing the heavy barrel against the man's face. The man's nose shattered. Blood sprayed into the air. The man let out a terror-filled squawk as he fell, his pants still bunched up around his ankles.

The other man sprang up from where he'd been holding the girl. He had an old Dragoon Colt pistol stuffed into his waistband and was tugging at it when Gabe pointed the Winchester at him and cocked the hammer. The man let his hand fall away from the pistol. "Hey, mister," he yelled, "I ain't done nothin' to you!"

Gabe slid off his horse, still keeping the man covered. "The fact that you're still alive is enough to bother the hell out of me," Gabe said, his voice cold and hard.

"But why?" the man demanded, a little angry now. "I never even seen you before. We got no reason to fight, mister."

Gabe jerked his chin toward the girl, who had rolled onto her side and was watching Gabe and the other man anxiously. "What you were doing to her," Gabe said, "that's reason enough to fight. Reason enough for any decent man to kill you."

The man's jaw dropped. "Are you serious?" he burst out. "Hell! She's only a damned Injun squaw! A Digger Injun!"

It was the man's tone that almost caused Gabe to shoot him, the man's genuine amazement that anyone could possibly believe that an Indian girl might have the same high feelings as a white girl. That she would honestly be horrified at the idea of being raped by two dirty, ignorant men. An image flashed through Gabe's mind, an image of his wife, Yellow Buckskin Girl, being shot down by a white cavalry officer. Of his mother being run through with a saber. By the same kind of human trash that stood before him now.

But people were already running from the fort, heading in Gabe's direction. Since the man in front of him had not drawn his gun, by the White Man's way of thinking, shooting him now might get Gabe hung. Instead he stepped in toward the man and, reversing his rifle, smashed the butt into the man's flushed, angry face. The man grunted, backpedaled, started to go down. Gabe stepped in closer, reversed the rifle once more, then raked the sharp front sight across the man's forehead, opening up a huge gash. The man fell, groaning. Lying on his back, he stared up at Gabe in confusion. A flap of loose skin hung half over his eyes. "Why?" he mumbled, then he passed out.

Gabe heard a cry. He turned. Three men were running toward him. Then Gabe heard another cry, much closer. Looking to the side, he saw that the girl, her face wild, was standing over the first man Gabe had knocked down, kicking him repeatedly in the groin. The man grunted through his ruined mouth, trying to crawl away, but the girl kept after him.

Gabe walked over and seized her by the wrist. She spun around, her eyes blazing. Gabe thought for a moment that she might turn on him next, so he said to her, in the language of Spotted Fawn's people, "Go, little sister. Go, before there is more trouble for you."

Surprise blotted out the anger on the girl's face. For a moment her features softened. "Go," he said again. She stared at him for a long moment, a moment of careful appraisal, now noticing those things about this stranger that were not quite white. This stranger who had saved her from being raped. Then, without a word, she darted away toward a stand of thick trees, holding her torn skirt around her lower body.

Gabe watched her go. He remembered the way she had fought to get away, he recalled the image of her kicking one of her attackers in the groin, and he smiled. A brave girl. A warrior's woman. A woman worth protecting.

CHAPTER THIRTEEN

Just as the girl disappeared into the trees, the three men who'd run over from the fort arrived. Gabe turned to face them, his rifle still in his hands, cocked and ready. He made no overt move to threaten the men; the rifle was threat enough.

The men came to a halt several yards away. Two of them were seedy-looking, dirty. The third was dressed a little better, and seemed, from his manner, to be in charge, although he was a nondescript man, looking a bit like a clerk. He had a pistol stuck into his waistband. The other two men also had pistols, although one appeared to be a single-shot, smooth-bore relic.

The leader glared at Gabe. "What the hell's going on here?" he demanded. He pointed down at the two would-be rapists Gabe had felled. "Why did you attack those men?"

"They were trying to rape a girl," Gabe replied coldly. "You must have seen it, I saw you looking this way."

The man seemed genuinely shocked. But not because of what the men had been doing. "What the hell?" he spluttered. "She was just a squaw."

"Yeah," one of the other men said, his voice as thin and mean as his face. "You done wrong, mister." He turned to his companions. "What say we put a coupla slugs in this yahoo, boys?"

Gabe raised the muzzle of the rifle a little. "Go ahead and try . . . it's up to you whether or not I have to kill you."

Defiance remained on the man's face for a second or two longer, then, facing Gabe's unwavering stare, and reading his own death there, he backed away a little, staring down at the ground mumbling, "Well . . . it just ain't right, what you done to those boys."

The leader was less cowed. "I'll have to ask you what the hell you're doing here," he said to Gabe. "This is an Indian reservation. No unauthorized white men allowed." He looked more closely at Gabe. "You *are* a white man, aren't you?"

Gabe did not answer the question but asked one of his own. "And what are you doing here?"

The man stood up a little straighter. "My name is Broaddus, J. L. Broaddus. I'm the Indian Agent. You're trespassing, mister. You could get yourself . . ."

Gabe jerked the muzzle of his rifle toward the two dazed and bleeding men lying on the ground. "And who are they? What are they doing here?"

"None of your business," Broaddus snapped. He eyed Gabe's rifle warily. "If you want to stay out of trouble, you'd better leave. . . ."

Gabe's face showed the contempt he felt. "So," he said softly, but not kindly, "you're the man who starves the people you're supposed to take care of. You're the man who sells what they produce and keeps the profit for his own use."

Broaddus's face colored. "I don't have to take that kind of talk. You get out of here. . . ."

"And those cattle I passed," Gabe continued. "What were they doing on Indian land, herded by non-Indians? Those are questions, Broaddus, that demand answers. And so far I haven't heard any."

Broaddus was now red as a beet. "Those cattle are here under lease," he snapped. "It's none of your damned business how I run this Agency."

Gabe was already walking toward his horse. "It's going to be. You can't keep starving these people, Broaddus.

You're going to have to start treating them as any human should be treated."

"Indians?" one of the other men asked incredulously.

"Like any person should be treated," Gabe repeated, swinging up into the saddle, with his rifle still in his right hand, pointed more or less in the direction of the others.

Broaddus took a step forward, anger having overcome any fear. "You must be new to these parts, mister," he said tightly. "I'll warn you once. Talking like that in Humboldt County is gonna buy you nothing but grief."

Gabe rode close to Broaddus and looked down at him. "I'll return the warning, Broaddus. Stop stealing from these people. Or I'll destroy you."

He started to ride away, then turned in the saddle. "One more thing," he added, pointing to the two men bleeding on the ground. "The girl that was attacked is not to be bothered. Tell those animals that if I ever see them near an Indian woman again, I'll kill them."

Again, the words were said so flatly that at first Broaddus did not understand their deadly intent. Until he looked once more into the stranger's cold, remorseless eyes, and as he did, he realized that the man would carry out his threat. Words died in Broaddus's throat as Gabe rode away. "Jesus," he muttered to himself. "I hope to hell he keeps on riding right on out of here."

Gabe left the reservation through the broad end of the valley. When he reached the main trail, he looked to his left, toward the east. If he rode far enough in that direction he knew he'd eventually come out of the mountains, into the upper portion of California's great central valley. From there, he could go in many directions. Perhaps it was time to leave this land of murder, robbery, and extortion. Humboldt County was not turning out to be the Eden he'd hoped for. There was too much death in this particular paradise.

But it would not be that easy to ride away. He thought of Spotted Fawn, living, almost an outcast, in a village that stood a good chance of being swallowed up in the storm of hatred and greed that was sweeping through the area. Also, he had promised Broaddus that he would make him pay for any more transgressions against the reservation Indians. He would not be able to keep that promise if he left.

So he turned his horse west. However, when he reached the entrance to Spotted Fawn's valley, he rode on past. He had things to do in Eureka. Things that concerned Spotted Fawn herself.

The girl had no real family. Worse, in her culture, she had no wealth, and she was blemished because of her earlier rape. There was only Salmon to protect her. Perhaps some man among the tribe would take her one day. Some very poor man. And Gabe had learned that, in Spotted Fawn's tribe, if a woman did not bring a high bride price, she was dishonored. And so were any children she might have. A stupid way for a people to think, but . . . since when had people been anything but stupid?

Gabe reached the coast late in the day. Not wanting to ride into Eureka at night, not wanting to stay in another seedy hotel, he bedded down in a small grove of redwoods, a tiny island of nature surrounded by a sea of devastation. All the land had been logged except for this one small grove, perhaps because it was in a cut, near a stream, and hard to get to.

In the morning he bathed himself in the stream. There might be fighting ahead, and if so, he wanted to enter the fighting purified. After breaking camp, he rode past Arcata, then down the wagon road toward Eureka. The air was as foul as before. He could smell Eureka long before he reached it.

He rode down the main street, looking at signs over storefronts. He had a great many things to buy. Then he saw two soldiers riding by. Gabe stopped his horse, watched the soldiers ride on out of town, heading south. He lost interest in his purchases. Instead, he followed the soldiers.

Salmon had talked about the soldiers, talked of them as a potent force in this land. A force that had sometimes helped, sometimes hurt the Red Man. But Salmon had never spoken of the soldiers with the hatred and loathing he reserved for the white settlers.

Perhaps there was something to be learned from the soldiers. Gabe followed the two troopers out past the edge of town. A mile further along, where the road narrowed, the soldiers stopped, then turned their mounts to face in Gabe's direction. He rode straight up to them.

"You followin' us, mister?" one of the soldiers asked coldly. His hand hovered near the open flap of his cavalry holster.

Gabe nodded. "I was hoping you were heading back to the fort. Is this the right direction?"

"Yeah," the soldier replied with a little less hostility. "What do you want at the fort? Not that many people come to see us. We ain't too popular around these parts."

"I'd like to talk to your commander."

The soldier's eyebrows rose. "Captain Johnson? You wanna see him?"

"Yes," Gabe replied. "I'd like to talk to him."

The other soldier grinned. "Well," he said, "I s'pose it's early enough in the day for the captain ta still be able ta talk."

"Shut up, Homer," the other soldier said, with no real heat in his voice. He turned toward Gabe. "Sure, mister. Might as well ride along with us."

The three men started off together, but Gabe noticed that the two soldiers kept a wary eye on him. There must be a great deal of mistrust between the citizenry and the troops. Gabe wondered if this Captain Johnson was a military tyrant. And what had the trooper meant when he'd said something about it being early enough for the captain to talk?

Gabe found out when they reached the fort. It was a rather rustic wooden place, constructed out of the local timber, overlooking the southern part of the bay. The troopers escorted him to a doorway, then rode off. Gabe dismounted, tied his horse to a hitching rail, then knocked on the door, which was made of heavy, rough planks. There was no answer at first, so he knocked again.

"Well, come on in, goddamn it," a voice called out from inside. "Before you knock the door down."

Gabe pushed open the door. A dimly lit room lay ahead of him. Half-closed shutters let in a weak ray of sunshine which cut a path through dancing dust motes. Then Gabe saw a man, seated on the far side of a desk, looking up at him lugubriously. The man had on a military jacket, with captain's bars on the shoulders. The coat was unbuttoned and did not look too clean, although it was hard to tell in this gloomy room.

The man continued to look at Gabe for several more seconds. Then he spoke. "Hey, you're a new one . . . haven't seen you around here before. What the hell jail did you break out of?"

Despite their meaning, there was no anger or sense of insult in the captain's words. Gabe looked more closely, then saw the bottle on the desk and the glass in the captain's hand. Now the trooper's words began to make sense, and Gabe wondered if, indeed, he'd gotten here early enough in the day.

The captain stood up, gestured to a chair. "Well, hell, go on and sit down, and tell me what brings you to this miserable hole."

Gabe sat. The captain plunked back down into his chair. Gabe watched him pour more whiskey into his glass. The bottle seemed to be about half full. That might be a good sign . . . unless it was not the first bottle of the day. "Want a drink?" the captain asked.

"No thanks."

The captain seemed a little relieved. Maybe whiskey was hard to get here. "My name's Johnson," the captain said. "What do I call you?"

"Gabe will do."

"First names, huh? Okay, tell you what. I call you Gabe, you call me Captain. Around here, that's my first name."

There was still no hostility in the captain's voice, more of an air of resigned gallows humor. The captain took another sip of his drink. Silence followed. Gabe got the impression it would continue on forever if he let it. "I was wondering," he finally said, "about the army's policy toward the local Indians."

"Huh!" the captain grunted. "There isn't any policy, as far as I can see. Unless you mean my own policy, and that's simple . . . leave them the hell alone, unless my superiors, sitting in happier places, tell me different."

The captain took a bigger sip. "Happier places," he muttered. "Happier than this sunless, isolated den of murderers."

He retreated into silence again. Gabe was wondering if he was going to have to prime the pump again, when the captain suddenly said, "Grant was here, you know."

"I beg your pardon?"

"Grant. Ulysses S. Grant. Sometime general and President. He was one of the first victims the army stationed out here, at the end of the known world. From what I understand, this is where Grant started his drinking." The captain looked mournfully at his glass. "I sure can understand that."

He looked back up at Gabe. "Anyhow, you asked me a question. I won't ask why you asked, but my answer still stands. I'd like to leave the poor bastards alone. They have enough trouble from Humboldt County's good and noble citizens, who butcher them for sport. Well, some of them do. Of course, they all want to get rid of the Indians, they all want their land. They just go about it in different ways. The more enlightened, most of them horny old bachelors, want to assimilate them, marry their women, get them to live like white people. There are others, probably the majority, who want to wipe them. Exterminate them like insects. Either way, the Indians lose, don't they?"

"I haven't seen much assimilation," Gabe replied.

"Well," the captain said, "maybe you rode by Indianola. A bunch of Indians have set up there, living White Man style, in White Man's housing, with regular streets, neat little lots. We Americans like everything to be square."

Gabe remembered the settlement he'd ridden by, between Arcata and Eureka. Indian people, white style houses.

"Not that it does 'em a lot of good," the captain said. "if somebody wants to kill 'em, or rape their women, they just go ahead and do it."

"Doesn't the law have anything to say about that?" Gabe asked.

The captain snorted. "Do anything to protect Indians? Our beloved sheriff? Hell, he's so crooked, he can sit two horses at once."

The captain looked critically at his glass. It was nearly empty. He glanced over at the bottle, but resisted the temptation. "Maybe you're wondering why I'm talking to you like this," he said. "Hell, after two years here, I talk to trees. Anything! Anybody! And you don't look like some of the yahoos I see in town. Or in the mountains. You asked me a question, so I'll tell you how it is with the Indians around here. They're on their way out. If they don't die fast enough from the White Man's diseases, they're helped along by bullets. Or knives. There was a big massacre back in sixty. I don't know if it was done to get rid of Indians, or just for fun. We've got some interesting types up here. That's why I asked what jail you broke out of. Up here, in the ass end of the world, we get a lot of people who are on the run, or just too mean to live in other places. They even have a name for 'em here . . . thugs. They're not only a social class, but a political power. The sheriff, rot his soul, is on their side. The few decent people keep their mouths shut . . . about the Indians, or anything else. Hell, that big newspaper fella, Bret Harte, lived in Arcata for a while. When he started writing articles about how bad the Indians were treated, the thugs sent him a message . . . get out of town. Or else. Not being all that stupid a man, Harte took the next steamer south."

"You mentioned a slaughter," Gabe cut in. "I know a little about that, but I also hear there was a war."

"Sure. A lot of Indians lost their whole families. They had nothing left to lose, so they went on the warpath. Took most of the county back for a while. That's when we were called in. No white men were ever punished for the murder of two hundred Indians, but the government sent us in to put down their rebellion. And we did. Killed some of them, too. But never just for the fun of it. If I discover a trooper with that kind of thinking, I give him lots of other things to think about. We don't shoot women and kids, either, like our noble local citizens. We fought our little war clean and fair, and when we finally won, we stuck the survivors on reservations. Not that the reservations do 'em much good."

Finally giving in, the captain poured another three fingers of whiskey into his glass, then sipped. "We had to keep the survivors here at the fort for a while. Had to build a big palisade around the women so the white men wouldn't rape them. That's a favorite sport around here. Raping and killing squaws. Hell, that palisade was eight feet high. And we had to sink it four feet into the ground to keep the bastards from tunneling underneath."

Remembering what he'd seen at the reservation, the attempted rape, Gabe nodded. The captain took this as a signal to continue. "Not that the Indians are completely innocent victims," he said. "They're a hard, tough people. When the first white men came through here . . . miners on their way to the mines on the Trinity River, the local Indians killed them out of hand. Real territorial people. Why, not too long ago, the government, in its infinite wisdom, moved one of the local tribes down south quite a ways. The tribe didn't like it there, so they broke out and tried walking back to their own country. The Indian tribes they passed along the way massacred all of 'em except one. A woman, if I recall. She musta been extra good at hiding."

Gabe nodded. Intertribal warfare was nothing new to him. Then, remembering Spotted Fawn's story, Gabe asked, "I hear some of the Indians are kidnapped."

"Oh yeah. Mostly kids. Take 'em away from their families, kill the parents if they resist. Maybe kill 'em anyhow, for fun. Then they sell the kids as indentured servants all over California and Nevada. The government tries to stop it, it's slavery, pure and simple, but it's a big area, with few people. The real thing, though, is land. The whites want the land and are bound and determined to get it. The Indians don't have the same idea of land ownership, they don't think of land as regular plots with artificial boundaries. They think of it as a valley, or some hilltops, where they hunt and fish and live. Hell, they haven't got a chance to hold onto their land, anyhow. You know, it's really only the government and the army that protects the Indians at all. And poorly. And it'll only get worse. Farming and ranching soaked up a lot of land, but now the lumber companies are moving in. By God, they want it all, every acre, every damned tree. And they got money behind 'em. Eastern money."

Captain Johnson looked at Gabe for a few seconds. "Maybe this is where I better ask why you're so interested in the Indians. You aren't working for some lumber company, are you? You aren't some hired gunman?"

Gabe shook his head. "I'm . . . living with some Indians. They're in a lot of trouble. I thought that if I knew more . . ."

Johnson nodded. "Yeah. You look like you might live with Indians. Reservation Indians?"

The captain's sharp question warned Gabe to be careful. "They used to be. They were starving on the reservation, so they left."

Johnson took a good-sized drink. "Yeah. The reservations. Run by thieves. I'm supposed to chase any runaways back onto the reservations, but I try to look the other way."

"I was just out at the Hoopa reservation," Gabe said. "I met a man named Broaddus. He was standing there, watching, while a couple of white men tried to rape a girl."

Captain Johnson scowled. "Ah, that damned Broaddus. He makes me ashamed of being white."

The captain looked up at Gabe. He was getting drunk, but there was still shrewdness in his eyes. "And the men who raped the girl?" he asked.

"Well . . . they *tried* to rape her," Gabe corrected. "I stopped them. Had to hurt them a little. Then I told Broaddus not to let it happen again."

Johnson let out a whoop of laughter. "Well, I'll be damned! I'd have loved to have seen that."

Then he grew serious. "But you better be careful. If you make enough enemies around here, you'll have a very short life. The thugs stick together. They're a rotten bunch. Watch out for one in particular. A man named Larrabee. He was one of the men who started the massacres. He kills for the sheer fun of it. And for profit, I suppose. You watch out for him."

Gabe nodded. "I will."

He let some time pass. "I saw a strange thing, out there on the reservation . . . a white cowboy running cattle. He said his boss had leased grazing rights on the reservation. Broaddus said the same thing."

Johnson slammed his glass down. "Damn!" he burst out. "I warned Broaddus not to do that again! He has no right!"

He looked up at Gabe. "Is he still selling Indian food?"

"So I hear."

Captain Johnson abruptly stood up. Gabe saw that he was really quite drunk now. He spilled some whiskey from his glass, then drank down the rest. "I warned that slimy snake," the captain said. "Now I'm gonna do something about it."

He stumped over to the door, tore it open. "Sergeant!" he bellowed. Through the doorway, Gabe saw a burly man in his middle years, with lots of chevrons on his sleeve, come walking over.

"Sir?" the sergeant asked.

"Saddle up B Troop. Full ammunition pouches, rations for two days. We ride in twenty minutes."

"Yessir," the sergeant replied, his face expressionless. Despite the captain's obvious drunkenness, Gabe thought he could detect just a touch of respect in the sergeant's manner.

The captain came back into the room. He began buckling on a pistol belt. Picking up a knapsack, he pushed the partially empty bottle of whiskey inside. "Trail rations," he grunted to Gabe.

"You're riding out to Hoopa, then?" Gabe asked.

"You bet your ass. You can ride along if you want. I'm gonna read the riot act to Broaddus. Make him get rid of those cattle."

"Do you have the right to do that?" Gabe asked.

The captain grinned. "Hell no. But with B Troop, I'll sure as hell have the power."

CHAPTER FOURTEEN

The cavalry troop rode out of the fort with a great clopping of hooves and jingling of metal. Gabe, riding at the front next to Captain Johnson, wondered how the horse soldiers had ever been able to sneak up on his people. But they had. Numerous times. At great cost in Indian lives. Viewpoint, Gabe reflected. That's what it was. The different manner in which each group looked at the world. There was little place in the Indian mind for the future. What would happen would happen. There was simply now, and when something bad happened, it would be dealt with at that time. Past, present, future, all three ideas were combined, all was a seamless whole.

Gabe had discovered that living in that nowness was a beautiful thing. But not particularly useful when it came time to deal with the White Man, who definitely had a concept of a future, who planned for future contingencies, then remorselessly carried out those plans, while an Indian warrior, even in the midst of battle, might decide to leave the fight and ride home for lunch.

Yes, the Indian way was a beautiful way to view the world, to view time. But ultimately a fatal one. Time after time small companies of white soldiers had defeated much larger Indian war parties.

White soldiers like the ones Gabe was riding with now. They were no braver, no more skillful at war than the

warriors Gabe had ridden with, but, as he rode along at
the head of the troop, he was aware of the training and
discipline all around him. Discipline that made an effec-
tive force out of the usual street scum that wound up in
the army.

And he was riding with them. Riding with the enemy.
Like some Crow warrior, riding scout, hunting down his tra-
ditional enemy, the Lakota. Riding with the power. Power
that would one day turn against his own people. But, power
is power, and that was what Gabe was using this troop for
now. Its power to coerce Agent Broaddus.

The troop clattered through Eureka without stopping,
then rode steadily along the wagon road past Arcata. As
Gabe had done, they turned inland at the mouth of the
same river. Captain Johnson told Gabe that it was called
the Mad River. "The first white men who came overland
to Humboldt County," he said, "camped on the banks of
the Mad. Some of them cracked up; it'd been a horrible
trip. A few of them starved to death. Didn't know how to
live off the land. So they call it the Mad. At least, I think
that's why."

Captain Johnson was chatty at first. Eventually either the
lack of a drink in his hand or perhaps a growing hangover
caused him to become taciturn. As the troop rode along, he
gazed morosely at the forest closing in around them, a vast
sea of trees, shutting this part of the state off from the more
civilized parts the captain seemed to prefer.

They could have reached the reservation by dark, but
the captain stopped the troop in the afternoon, in a grassy
meadow ringed by huge trees. "I don't want to ride in there
too late in the day," the captain explained to Gabe as an
orderly was setting up his tent. "I want to have the whole
day to tear Broaddus a new asshole. We'd miss too much
in the dark."

Gabe had to admit that was good planning. Now that
Johnson was closer to his objective and engaged in active
planning, he seemed to perk up. Gabe watched him walking
around the little encampment, positioning tents, posting the
first round of lookouts. Gabe, who had no tent to pitch,

already had his bedroll laid out on the ground.

Gabe became aware of someone standing next to him. He turned. It was the big sergeant. His faded blue eyes were following the captain. His weather-beaten face held an expression Gabe could only interpret as affection.

The sergeant saw that Gabe was watching him. "He's a good officer," he said abruptly. "A good man. It's just that he doesn't have anything to do with himself up here."

Both Gabe and the sergeant watched the captain, who had discovered some fault with a trooper's gear. "What he needs," the sergeant said, "is a war. A real war."

He started to turn away, toward a malingering trooper, but then turned back to look toward the captain. "Or maybe no war at all," he added grudgingly.

They rode onto the reservation a little before ten in the morning. "Plenty of daylight," the captain said gleefully. "We'll be able to see every rotten thing that miserable shit is doing."

The twenty-five troopers were quickly deployed. "Sergeant," the captain ordered, "take ten men. Go round up all the cattle you can find and bring them back here, along with any white men herding them."

By the time the sergeant and his detail rode away, Broaddus had become aware of the troops. He came shambling out of his little fort, pulling his suspenders up over a dirty shirt. Gabe caught sight of an Indian girl in the doorway behind him. She had a blanket pulled half around her body. Otherwise, she appeared to be naked. He studied her for signs of abuse, but she looked despairing rather than frightened.

Broaddus looked plain confused. Picking up speed, he headed toward Captain Johnson, who was sitting his horse calmly, waiting. Gabe noticed that, with Broaddus out of the way, the Indian girl had left the doorway and was heading toward the tree line. Gabe's anger rose. He supposed the girl had little choice but to allow herself to be used by Broaddus. Perhaps he paid her with some of the food he stole from her people.

"What . . . what the hell are you doing here, Johnson?" Broaddus burst out. "How come you're bringing soldiers onto Agency land?"

"I heard there was trouble here," the captain responded. "Trouble with the Indians. That's what the army's been stationed in Humboldt County for, isn't it? To prevent Indian trouble?"

"There's no damn trouble here!" Broaddus spluttered. "If there had been, I'd have called for you. . . ."

Then Broaddus saw Gabe, on the captain's far side. His voice died away, and his skin changed color, a shade somewhere between pale fear and ruddy fury. Captain Johnson saw where Broaddus was looking, but he pretended to see nothing. Instead, he gazed around the area, placidly. "Is that a storehouse over there?" he asked Broaddus, pointing toward a heavily constructed log building.

"Why, uh . . . yeah."

"Is that where you store the provisions that come in for the Indians? And the food they grow for themselves?"

"Uh, well . . ."

The captain shook his head. "Always a tactical mistake, Broaddus . . . to overcentralize your most valuable resources."

"I don't understand . . ." Broaddus muttered, his face now a sickly green. He already suspected what was going to happen.

"In civilian terms," the captain said, almost amiably, "it's called having all your eggs in one basket. Hell, what if there were a fire? Or the creek rose? You'd lose everything."

He looked straight at Broaddus now, and the good humor disappeared. Broaddus looked away, unable to meet the captain's relentless gaze. "It'd be a shame if something happened to those supplies," the captain snapped. "Then the Indians would have nothing to eat. You wouldn't like that to happen, would you, Broaddus? The Indians being your responsibility and all."

"I . . ."

"Fine. Let's go over and see what you've got."

"Hey, look!" Broaddus said desperately. "You haven't got the right to—"

"I do if there's danger of an Indian problem," the captain replied, his voice flat. "And hungry Indians could make for a real bad problem."

He and Gabe and two troopers rode over to the storehouse. The other troopers stayed behind. The same two men Gabe had seen on his earlier visit had come out of the Agency headquarters and were now standing near Broaddus, shifting nervously from foot to foot. Gabe, remembering his conversation with the captain, wondered what jail they might have broken out of. Maybe they were wondering if certain wanted posters had finally made it all the way to Humboldt.

The storehouse door was locked. Broaddus was trotting in their direction, his face a mask of frustrated anger. "Do you have the key?" the captain asked when Broaddus finally came panting up to them.

"No. It's . . . been lost."

The captain shrugged, then drew his revolver. "Guess we'll just have to shoot it open, then."

"Wait!" Broaddus shouted. The door was secured by an obviously expensive padlock. Broaddus fumbled through a series of pockets, trying to make it look like he didn't know where the key was. He finally came up with one. "Maybe this'll work," he muttered.

He opened the lock, but made no move to open the door. Captain Johnson swung down from his horse and opened the door himself. "My, my," he said, peering inside. "So much stuff. These lucky redskins are sure living off the fat of the land."

The irony of the captain's statement hung in the air. A number of Indians, having heard about the soldiers, perhaps from the girl who'd walked away into the woods, were beginning to gather. They were emaciated. Their ribs showed, their bellies were distended. For the first time, Gabe saw anger tug at the captain's features. "Broaddus," he murmured, "I'm tempted to hang you. Right here, right now."

Broaddus flared. "You can't! You got no right to . . . you got no rights over me. I work for—"

"Shut up!" the captain suddenly roared. "Before I call for a rope!"

Broaddus swallowed, turned a ghastly shade of gray. Gabe doubted that the captain would actually hang Broaddus. Apparently Broaddus wasn't so sure, and he undoubtedly knew the captain a lot better than Gabe did.

Johnson signaled for the watching Indians to come nearer. Several moved toward the storehouse. Gabe was impressed. Indians usually went to great lengths to stay out of the way of soldiers. But, considering Broaddus, soldiers were probably a considerably lesser evil. Or maybe it was the lure of all that food, until now locked away, out of their reach.

"Any of you speak English?" the captain asked.

A young woman came forward. Gabe saw that it was the girl who'd almost been raped the last time he'd been here. "Little bit," she said haltingly. She looked fleetingly at Gabe.

"You tell this to your people, then," the captain said. He gestured toward the storehouse's open door. "You tell them to take what's in there. Take it to your houses. Take all of it."

Fear of loss immediately overcame Broaddus's fear of death. "Wait!" he screamed. "You can't do that! Why . . . why, my staff and I . . . we won't have anything left to eat!"

Captain Johnson smiled at Broaddus, a cold, merciless smile. "Well, then,"—he waved around at the Indians— "maybe you could ask these good people for a handout."

Broaddus had to watch helplessly while the Indians, obviously quite excited, began emptying the storehouse. The place was packed to the roof. Gabe got the impression that this couldn't have happened at a worse time for Broaddus; apparently he'd been accumulating all these supplies for some time, probably readying them for sale. Gabe watched Broaddus's face as the stock steadily diminished. More and more Indians were showing up, cleaning out the storehouse the way ants clean out an unguarded cupboard. Broaddus actually looked as if he were going to be sick. How greed captures some men, Gabe thought disgustedly.

But now Broaddus was facing even greater problems. The sergeant and his patrol were returning with a herd of about twenty-five bawling cattle. "Wait!" Broaddus burst out again. "What are they doing with those cattle?"

"The same thing as with the supplies," Johnson replied. He bent forward in the saddle, looking past the troopers, to where a dejected cowboy, the same one Gabe had met earlier, was glumly watching his charges being led away. "My word," the captain said mildly. "You've done a great job here, Broaddus. Your Indians are so rich they can afford to hire white cowboys to herd their cattle."

"But . . . those aren't their . . ." Broaddus started to say. There was no point in finishing the sentence. Either they were Indian cattle, or they were here illegally. He could only stare at the cattle, in obvious pain, wondering how he was going to explain all this to the white man who actually owned them. Or *had* owned them. He cringed as he heard the captain say to the girl, who was still interpreting, "You might be better off to slaughter these animals right away, and dry the meat. Cattle have ways of disappearing."

The girl nodded eagerly. Her mouth was already watering at the thought of big chunks of juicy meat. As she went off to spread the news, the captain walked toward the cattle, perhaps to read their brands. Gabe dismounted, then moved close to Broaddus. "As I told you the last time," he said softly to the Agent, "if there are any reprisals against these people . . . I won't bother with hanging. I'll just cut your guts out."

As before, Gabe's words were spoken without heat, less of a threat, more of a calm, unshakable promise. Broaddus felt his guts, the ones mentioned, churn with fear. But, for just a moment, his rage won out over his fear. He knew who had set up this whole disastrous raid on his illicit livelihood. "You're gonna be a marked man, mister," he hissed. "There'll be men looking for you all over this county."

Gabe didn't answer, just continued to look Broaddus straight in the eye. Finally, Broaddus looked away, then shuffled off, confused and dispirited. Captain Johnson came over to watch him go. "Well," Gabe said to the captain, "I suppose that's that."

To his surprise, Captain Johnson shook his head. "No. Nothing's really changed. We won a battle, but eventually men like Broaddus will win the war. He'll send off a blast of shit to the government department he works for back in Washington. They hate the army, all those bureaucrats hate each other. They figure if one of them gets a little power, it'll diminish their own power. And power is money. The other way around, too, I guess. The old story of the chicken and the egg. No matter. They'll fry my ass for this, and Broaddus will be riding high again."

"It's all for nothing, then?" Gabe demanded.

The captain shrugged. "I wouldn't say that."

He gestured toward the Indians. The last of them were staggering away under loads of supplies. Others were driving the doomed cattle. "At least they'll eat well for a while."

He turned toward Gabe, smiled mirthlessly. "And what the hell can they do to punish me? Exile me to Fort Humboldt?"

CHAPTER FIFTEEN

They left the reservation in the late afternoon, after making certain that the supplies and cattle were so securely in the hands of the Indians—indeed, were even now being eaten ravenously—that Broaddus would not be able to get them back. "Of course," Captain Johnson said as he rode alongside Gabe, "Broaddus will start stealing again, but it'll take him a little while to get up the guts to steal so much."

Now that the action was over, Johnson sank back into his usual torpor. However, it wasn't until the troop had bedded down for the night, near the river, that the captain took out his bottle again. Solace, of a sort, Gabe figured, but at the cost of the man's soul.

The next morning, they got a late start; the captain did not seem eager to get moving. He spent an hour checking the men's gear, their trail readiness. He did not seem to be doing it out of a sense of efficiency, but more as a petulant burst of frustration. Gabe suspected he had a hangover.

They reached Eureka a little before noon. Here Gabe and the troop parted company. Gabe and the captain shook hands while they were still a mile out of town. "Thanks for what you did," Gabe told Johnson, and meant it.

A sort of spasm passed over the captain's face. "I wish I could do more," he murmured. Then he gave an order to the sergeant, who gave an order to the troop, and they started off again. Gabe let them ride ahead of him. He had decided to enter town alone; he had already identified himself too closely with the local army garrison.

As Gabe rode down Eureka's main street, the only sign that the troop had passed through town were a few piles of steaming horse droppings. Gabe headed straight for a livery stable. After a little haggling, he purchased a small, rather old horse as a pack animal, along with a battered army packsaddle. He left his new packhorse with the hostler, but saddled and bridled and ready to ride. Then he headed back into the center of town on foot, with his black stallion happily munching oats in a livery stall, also saddled and bridled.

Over the next two hours Gabe bought a large number of items, dipping deep into his stock of gold coins. Each time he purchased all that he could carry, he walked back to the livery stable and loaded the goods onto the packhorse, which, being old, with lots of experience in involuntary servitude to the human race, accepted the weight resignedly.

After lashing the last load into place, Gabe decided to go back out onto the street one more time. He had been deliberating over one particular item, a slender gold chain from which dangled a particularly lovely cameo, a carved head of some Greek goddess. How such an item had reached these shores, he did not know.

After examining the chain and cameo one last time, he bought it, had it placed in a nice little box, and shoved the box into the empty right pocket of his duster. He felt good about the purchase, thought it the perfect complement to the more practical items he had been buying so far. Unfortunately, his absorption in the pleasure of his purchase made him less attentive to his surroundings than normal. He was about halfway to the livery stable when he heard someone cry out, "Hey! That's him! That's the bastard!"

Looking in the direction from which the cry had come, Gabe was surprised to see the two men who had been at the reservation with Broaddus. Another man was with them, a tall, rangy man with one of the hardest faces Gabe had ever seen. No, maybe hard wasn't a strong enough word. Mean. Vicious. Without any kindness or nobility at all.

One of the men from the reservation was babbling away at this man. "He's the one I told you about, Larrabee. The one that busted up Zeke and Larkin, then brought the army out to rob ol' Broaddus blind."

Larrabee. Gabe had heard that name before. Yes. Captain Johnson had mentioned him. One of the thugs, one of the criminals who dominated Humboldt County. And maybe one of the men who'd led the massacre of the Indians a few years back.

Considering all the goods he had just bought, and what he intended doing with them, Gabe would have preferred avoiding a fight and riding on out of this miserable town. But, if this Larrabee was the one he thought he was, that would not do. Better a confrontation now. Gabe addressed the man who'd been babbling. "If you have something to say about me, mister . . . better say it directly to my face."

The man spun toward him, smirking. No more cringing, as at the reservation. Apparently, Larrabee's presence was stiffening his backbone. "You don't scare me none, Injun lover," he snarled. "You was a big man when you had all the hardware, but you don't look so damn big now."

Gabe ignored him. The one to watch was Larrabee. He was packing a six-shooter, low on his right hip. A gun-fighter's rig. Larrabee was looking straight at him, the smallest of smiles tugging at his thin lips. "You made a mistake, mister," Larrabee said. His voice was thin and cold, like his face. But not very strong. Gabe had expected more deadliness in the man's voice.

"You messed up bad, coming into town without the army protecting you," Larrabee continued. "It's the last mistake you're gonna make, 'cause we're gonna kill you, you Indian-lovin' son of a bitch."

Larrabee glanced over at the two men with him. "Spread out, boys. We'll all go together."

A fight, then, Gabe thought. Three against one. Bad odds, particularly when one of his opponents was a man with Larrabee's reputation. He tensed, ready to move, watching the three men close in on him. They were not fanning out as Larrabee had suggested, but were coming on fairly well bunched together. That might help.

There was something wrong here, something out of kilter, something that he'd better consider if he was going to walk away alive. For one thing, Larrabee had let himself lag a little behind the other two men. So far Gabe had concentrated most of his attention on Larrabee, as the most deadly of the three. Now he realized that, while Larrabee might be a killer, he was also crafty. Perhaps even cowardly. He was letting the other two men screen him. He'd shoot from behind them, letting them draw any initial fire. Smart. But rotten, lacking courage.

Gabe shifted his attention back to the other two men. Barely in time. Confident in being backed up by a man like Larrabee, although they didn't seem to be aware of how far back he really was, they both reached for their guns at the same moment, one of them screaming, "I'll blow your guts out, you son of a bitch!"

Stupid bravado, that wild cry, perhaps making the man feel more courageous, but also slowing his draw, ruining his aim.

Gabe was wearing both his pistols, one beneath his right arm, the other on his right hip. He drew them both together, while at the same time stepping quickly to his right. Holding both pistols high, but not really aiming, not at this distance—he and his opponents were only separated by a few yards—Gabe opened fire at about the same time as the others.

Bullets passed through the spot where he'd been standing. Gabe fired rapidly, knowing that at least two of the men he was facing were not real gunmen, that the roar of his pistols, the flash and flame and smoke from their muzzles, plus the horrible knowledge that those pistols were aimed straight at them, might cause the reservation men to fire wildly.

It did. Howling with fear now, lips pulled back tight over their teeth, the two men from the reservation scattered lead all over the street. Not Gabe. Of his first six shots, three hit the two men. One was hit in the throat and the shoulder. The other caught a ball in the gut. Both stayed on their feet, but both were effectively out of the fight.

Which left Larrabee. But Larrabee was suddenly no longer a target. He had drawn later than the other two men, apparently in no hurry, ready to finish Gabe off even if his slowness cost the lives of the others. But he had not expected the volume of lead Gabe was now aiming at Larrabee and his cronies. So, like the others, Larrabee fired too quickly. He watched the other two men reel backward, then begin to fall, and now those two blazing pistols held by the big man with the cold eyes were tracking toward him. Initially confident— after all, he was in his own environment, his own town— Larrabee now began to have doubts. The terrible sureness, the total lack of fear with which this stranger had faced three armed men, the coolness with which he'd so far shot two of them half to pieces, and the deadliness of his manner as he turned toward the single survivor, himself, suggested to Larrabee that he'd made a mistake by not coming after this man with the odds even more in his favor.

Gabe had already tried a shot at Larrabee, but he'd had to shoot past the two men he'd already hit, and his shot missed. Now Larrabee was fading to the side, moving toward the entrance to an alley, still screening himself with the bodies of the other two. But they would not remain in the way for long. The one who'd been hit in the throat was slowly strangling, turning blue in the face, about to fall. The one with the stomach wound was toppling forward, his arms clasped over his guts, shrieking in pain.

But Larrabee was already ducking into the alley. He turned at the last moment, partly screened by the corner of a building, and fired at Gabe, but, once again, too quickly. His bullet burned its way through the air a few inches from Gabe's left ear, then Gabe was firing again, sending three quick shots at Larrabee. The bullets gouged splinters from the wooden building. Blinking, the skin of his face burning from the splinters, Larrabee ducked back into the alley. Gabe waited. No movement. With both pistols cocked, he moved closer to the alley, but Larrabee did not reappear.

Gabe halted. Running into that alley entrance when he was not sure just where Larrabee might be could get him shot. Also, after so much firing, his pistols were nearly empty. He ducked into a doorway, stuffed one pistol back into his belt holster, then quickly slipped the cylinder out of the other pistol. Only one shot left. He dropped the cylinder into his right coat pocket. Next to the cameo and chain, he realized. No time to think about that now. He reached into his left coat packet and pulled out a loaded cylinder. Good, the caps were all in place. It took only a few seconds to slip the cylinder into the pistol's frame.

He repeated the operation with the other pistol. He now had another dozen shots. What he wished most was that he had his rifle. Only a fool preferred a pistol over a rifle.

He flattened himself against the building next to the alley, then quickly poked the side of his face around the corner. All he saw was an empty alley. However, there were plenty of doorways where Larrabee could be hiding, even other alleys branching off to the left and right. Going down that alley without knowing where Larrabee was hiding was pretty close to suicide.

Besides, the shooting had brought on a great commotion, shouts of surprise and alarm. Gabe heard booted feet pounding along the boardwalk to his right. The shots would bring men, and perhaps the law, and Gabe had little doubt as to his popularity in a place like Eureka.

Also, Larrabee might be circling around behind him. Then there was the reason he had come into town in the first place. His purchases. If he did not get to the livery stable quickly he might lose not only the packhorse, but his stallion and his rifles as well.

Gabe thrust both pistols back into their holsters, then walked quickly away, toward his left, toward the livery stable. He passed half a dozen armed men, running toward where he'd shot it out with Larrabee and his cronies. "What happened?" a burly logger carrying a shotgun shouted at Gabe, reassured by the fact that the only gun visible on this stranger was riding securely in a holster. "Are the fuckin' Injuns attackin'?"

Gabe shook his head. "No. Just some drunks having it out."

The men ran on past him. Gabe made it to the livery stable without incident. He flipped the hostler half a dollar, mounted his black, took hold of the packhorse's lead rope, and rode out the rear of the livery stable. Since Eureka was not very large and still quite rude, he was out of town and into the ravaged woods behind it within less than a minute.

He circled around the town, making certain that he was screened from view all the way. He could hear a lot of shouting from the town, along with the neighing of horses. Perhaps there would be a pursuit. He was glad he'd chosen to ride out the south end of town. If they followed, they'd head in that direction, but Gabe doubted they'd follow at all, no matter what kind of story Larrabee concocted. There had been a few witnesses. They must have seen the two men from the reservation draw first. And Larrabee, who had acted like a coward, like a back-shooter, like the kind of man who would hack helpless Indian women and children to death, would have to be careful what he said, or he'd come out of this looking bad.

Still, Gabe would no longer be able to move around the area so openly. Small loss. He had no use for Eureka. He had a much finer place to head for . . . the village of Spotted Fawn and her people.

Damned if he'd be in a big hurry to leave that lovely, peaceful little valley.

CHAPTER SIXTEEN

When Gabe returned to the village there was a great deal of curiosity concerning his packhorse, and the mountain of material piled on the packsaddle. The possibility of gifts entered a number of minds.

Salmon came out of his sweat lodge with his two friends. Gabe saw Spotted Fawn slip out through the entrance of her house. Her face glowed with delight and relief when she saw Gabe, but, when he made no move toward her, the girl's face fell.

Gabe met Salmon right in the middle of the village. "You see that I have brought many things," he said, pointing toward the packhorse.

"I see," Salmon replied, nodding cautiously.

"I wish to give them to you."

Surprised, Salmon pointed to his breast and asked, "To me? All that?"

"Yes," Gabe replied. "in exchange for your niece, Spotted Fawn."

Gabe hesitated for a moment. "Will you accept my gifts?" he asked, no longer quite so sure of what he was doing. Perhaps he was violating some taboo. Perhaps he was going about this all wrong. In a Lakota camp he'd know what to do, know how many horses he would have to give for a woman as lovely as Spotted Fawn.

There was a moment's answering hesitation on Salmon's

face, then a huge smile split his features. His hesitation had not been from doubt, but from sheer amazement. "I accept!" he cried.

Gabe turned, solemn-faced, and began to unload the packsaddle. He glanced over at Spotted Fawn; she was still standing next to her house, stunned, seemingly unable to move. Salmon saw her, too. "Get over here, woman," he ordered. "Help your man unload his horse."

She moved then, coming over to Gabe. Her face showed awe, wonder, amazement. She began to help empty the packsaddle, although she was barely aware of what she was unloading; her eyes remained locked on Gabe the whole time.

"No," Gabe told her as she started to place a large cooking pot in front of Salmon. "That is for you. As are many other things."

He pulled a thick blanket out of the pack and placed it with the pot. Two piles grew, one for Salmon, one for Spotted Fawn. He did not know if this was customary, but he was not going to permit Spotted Fawn to remain a pauper. Her house would be richly stocked.

One of his gifts to Salmon was a Winchester rifle, like his own. Salmon handled the weapon in wonder. "It is not for deer," Gabe said, straight-faced. "It is for shooting men who disturb this village."

Salmon, remembering their bow hunt of the deer, laughed heartily as he worked the Winchester's loading lever. Gabe laughed with him, and now the mood lifted. When the last item had been removed from the packsaddle, Gabe handed the animal's reins to Salmon. "The horse, too, is yours."

Salmon took the reins, stunned. "So many riches," he murmured. "So much."

"No," Gabe replied. "So little for what I receive in return."

He took Spotted Fawn by the hand. She looked down in confusion, but he could see the flush of delight on her lovely face, sense the tears of joy in her eyes.

Looking up, Gabe caught sight of Broken Bow, standing several yards away. The older man's expression was a mixture of shock and horror. For a moment Gabe wondered why, then he realized that Broken Bow was probably no longer the richest man in the village. Salmon, the former pauper, had usurped him. Good, Gabe thought. He fervently hoped that Salmon would handle wealth with a little more humility than Broken Bow.

There was one more gift. Gabe reached into his coat pocket and pulled out the little box. Opening it, he removed the gold chain and cameo. He fumbled with the clasp, finally got it open, then put it around Spotted Fawn's neck. When he stepped back, the cameo glowed against the girl's dark skin, just where the deep cleft between her breasts began. She looked down, studying the carving on the cameo, and when she finally looked up, straight into Gabe's eyes, all her hesitation and shyness were gone. "I am yours now," she said softly.

There was a ceremony the next day, in which Spotted Fawn officially became Gabe's wife. He had brought many store trinkets to adorn her. She literally tinkled when she walked. Gabe and Salmon had ridden out early to the area of bald hills where Salmon, to his great delight, had shot a deer with his new rifle. Gabe shot one, too. There was more than enough meat for the feasting that followed the ceremony.

Now came the problem of separate quarters. Gabe wanted to immediately make love to his new wife. Spotted Fawn seemed just as eager. But both had to wait until the festivities distracted everyone's attention, then Gabe and the girl slipped away into the forest, carrying one of the blankets he had brought her from Eureka.

They made love in the open, under a high canopy of redwood trees, with a soft carpet of redwood needles beneath the blanket. She clung to him afterward, her face shining with joy. Then the joy faded a little. "You will not leave someday?" she asked anxiously.

"Not without you."

He had already thought about this. He did not know if he would be able to stand the sedentary life of Spotted Fawn's village for too long. Perhaps he would take the girl to his own people, to the Lakota reservation. She would be much safer there than here, on those occasions when he chose to ride out on his own. Because he was not a man who could live without wandering.

Then he remembered Two Rivers. What would happen if he brought back a strange woman to the Oglala village?

Besides, he was aware of the difficulties of traveling long distances with a girl who was obviously an Indian. He'd be all right, he could wear his white man's clothing on the trail. She might wear a white woman's dress, but she would always be identifiable as an Indian. He wondered if she would like the Plains.

He would try it. Perhaps they might go live on the Cheyenne reservation. He had no wish to hurt Two Rivers. Of course, perhaps he could take Two Rivers for a second wife. Would the two women get along? There were obviously many problems inherent in marriage.

He would worry about all that later. Today was today. Gabe sighed in contentment as he and Spotted Fawn lay together on the blanket, both naked after making love, each absentmindedly touching the other's body.

Spotted Fawn sat up and began tracing her fingers over the long, thin scars on Gabe's chest and arms. She had seen them before, of course, but now she was beginning to feel proprietary. "What made these?" she asked.

"I did."

She looked surprised.

"When my wife and my mother were killed."

He hesitated. "It is a custom of my people."

"Of course," she replied. "I sometimes forget that you are not really a white man."

He hesitated, but then continued. "We had been married only a few days, my wife and I. We had left our own village to visit the village where my mother and her husband were visiting relatives. Soldiers . . . attacked the village."

Gabe fell silent for a few seconds, remembering. There had been warnings of soldiers in the area. Gabe had brought one of those warnings. But he was not believed, partly because he had been living at the fort for several years. Some believed him to be a spy for the White Man. So no special guard had been set. No patrols sent out.

He could have done the patrolling himself. But he was too wrapped up in his new wife, too absorbed in seeing his mother again, after the years of separation. After the nightmare of the fort, of prison.

"They attacked very early in the morning," he told Spotted Fawn. "When most of the People were still asleep. I was up early; I fired some of the first shots in defense of the village. But it was too little, too late. The soldiers came riding into the village, killing, killing. They killed men, women, old people, children. I was trying to save two babies when a soldier attacked my wife and my mother. They had just come out of a lodge. The soldier shot my wife in the stomach first, then in the head. She fell dead. Then the soldier thrust his saber through my mother's chest. She died more slowly."

Gabe did not add that the soldier had been his enemy from the fort, Captain Stanley Price. The man Gabe had bested twice in fights. Gabe had gone to the guardhouse for winning one of those fights. Three years locked away from the sun and light and air. During the second fight, shortly after Jim Bridger had got him out of the guardhouse, Gabe had broken his right index finger on the captain's jaw. He had not been able to close his fist tightly enough, because, a few moments before, the captain had stuck the tine of a pitchfork through his palm.

The attack on the village had been made by the army, but Gabe had never been able to get over the feeling that the death of his wife and mother had been his fault. His fault for not killing Price when he'd had the chance. How foolish to leave an enemy alive!

Price was a hater, a man given over totally to revenge. During the attack on the village, he'd recognized Amelia Conrad, with her gray-streaked golden hair, as Gabe's mother. And the Indian girl with Amelia as someone important to Gabe. Gabe had watched both killings, had watched in horror as Captain Price killed the two women. Price had locked eyes with Gabe a moment before, seen the anguish on his face.

Gabe had been able to do nothing. He'd had a baby under

each arm, ready to ride them away from the soldiers. When he'd finally reached his pistol, it had misfired. He had been helpless, separated from Price and his victims by knots of fighting, struggling people. He could only watch as Price killed.

"We fought hard," Gabe said to Spotted Fawn, his voice distant. "Many escaped, guarded by the warriors. But the soldiers were still in the camp. And while they were there, they burned the lodges, destroyed the food and supplies. Destroyed all that was meant to keep the People alive during the winter. They wanted all of the People to die, to starve and freeze. So that the white men could take over an empty land."

Gabe looked down at the scars on his arms. "Later, I cut myself with my knife, to show my grief. I put my wife on a platform, the Lakota way. My mother I put in the ground, in the manner of her people."

Spotted Fawn sat next to him, subdued. "Your people, then, suffered as much as ours."

"Perhaps."

Gabe said nothing about his long hunt to track down Stanley Price. The final showdown at a barn on an isolated ranch. Price, running from the burning barn, the barn Gabe had lit on fire, Price engulfed in flames, screaming to be shot. Gabe, feeling no mercy, letting him burn. The snow melting around Price's scorched corpse.

If I'd only killed him before, when I had the chance, Gabe thought again. For the thousandth time. Then the women might not have died.

He tore himself away from the past, looked at the girl sitting next to him, naked, legs tucked beneath her body, her eyes downcast.

He placed his fingers beneath her chin, made her look up at him. "I have a new woman now," he said softly. Then he added silently, just for himself, the way he'd heard the white men put it . . . for better or for worse.

But she had heard only his spoken words, and her face lighted with joy. "I am yours forever," she replied, reaching out to touch his face. Almost with wonder.

CHAPTER SEVENTEEN

The summer continued. Once more the village camped by the larger river, a good time for Gabe and Spotted Fawn, who were able to spend a great deal of time making love in the woods. Night after night they lay together, wrapped in Spotted Fawn's new blankets, each very aware of the warmth of the other's body.

Fall arrived. Some mornings there was a sharp nip in the air. The tribe moved back to the village. Now, Spotted Fawn was expected to sleep in her house. Gabe slept in the sweat lodge with Salmon and his friends. From time to time Gabe and Spotted Fawn slipped off into the woods to be alone. Gabe was not happy with the situation, but Spotted Fawn, having been brought up in this tradition, accepted it tranquilly.

The days began to drag for Gabe. Once again he thought of taking Spotted Fawn back to his people, the Lakota. He mentioned it to her once. She became uneasy. Except for her earlier kidnapping, she had never lived away from her people, or from these inland valleys. Her people were sedentary. So was she.

Gabe began riding out from the village more and more often. Sort of a patrol, at least, that's the way he explained it to Spotted Fawn. Yet, she was aware of his restlessness and grew increasingly sad. One day she mentioned, on her own, the prospect of both of them riding far away. But he could see that her heart was not in it. She had finally reached the goal of the average young woman of her culture . . . a fine husband, in fact, an outstanding husband, a hero among her people, plus a solid house, and a certain amount of material wealth. Given her own way, Spotted Fawn would have preferred the situation to continue just as it was. Forever.

One morning, more restless than usual, Gabe saddled his stallion, slipped his rifles into their scabbards, belted a pistol around his bare waist, and rode away from the village. It was a beautiful day, the bright sunshine felt good on Gabe's bare skin. It was not as hot as it had been, but still warm enough for him to be wearing only moccasins and a breechclout. If it grew cold later, he would ride back to the village.

He rode south and a little east, into another valley, a broader valley than the one in which Spotted Fawn's people lived. Salmon had told Gabe that another group of their larger tribe had left the reservation and settled in this area. Perhaps he would ride into the village and see how they were doing.

He rode carefully; barging into someone else's territory, especially in times like these, was always dangerous. Perhaps the first thing this other group would see would be his light hair and eyes, and they would shoot first and ask questions later.

He was riding near a stream when he heard gunshots about a quarter mile ahead, mixed with screams of fear and agony. He immediately stopped his horse and listened. There were no more shots, but still a few screams, fainter this time.

Nudging his horse, he cantered carefully in the direction from which the shots had come. The land opened out a little, there were more meadows, fewer trees, so that he was able to see two people lying on the ground near a small stream. Indians.

He halted. Nothing else moved. Then one of the Indians stirred, moaned. Gabe rode closer, keeping alert, his eyes scanning the terrain all around.

A man and a woman lay on the ground. They were dressed like Spotted Fawn's people. Both had been shot. The man appeared to be dead, but the woman stirred again, groaned. Gabe slipped off his horse, but held the reins firmly as he knelt next to the woman. He saw that she was young, but that she was unlikely to live long. She had been shot in the center of her chest, between her breasts, which were bare like Spotted Fawn's. The woman, sensing someone above her, opened her eyes. Fear contorted her features as she looked into Gabe's light gray eyes.

"Do not be afraid," he said softly, in the tongue of Spotted Fawn's people.

She understood. "You," she murmured weakly. "You are the white man who lives with our people."

He nodded, stroked his hand along her cheek for comfort. "Tell me what happened," he said. "Who shot you?"

The woman turned her head, saw the man lying next to her, motionless. Grief tore at her features.

Then, alarm. She stared wildly into the distance and tried to sit up, but she was too weak and fell back helplessly.

"Rest," Gabe said, stroking her forehead. There was nothing he could do except not let her die alone.

The woman twisted her head wildly, her eyes desperate. "My children!" she gasped.

"What children?" Gabe asked, looking around for other bodies. "Where are they?"

"White men," she murmured. "Took our children. Took them to be slaves. Shot my husband when he fought back. Shot me when they tried to rape me and I fought them with a knife."

The woman tried to raise her head again, to look for her children, Gabe supposed. Then a great gout of blood burst from her mouth, and she fell back, dead.

Gabe slowly stood up. My God, what was the matter with this land? His own land was not a soft one, but this apparent paradise, this Eden, was the most vicious place he'd ever seen. He felt rage stirring within him, but beat it down, controlled it, let it solidify into a cold, implacable desire to salvage some kind of justice from this tragedy.

The first thing was to get the children back. Mounting his horse, he left the two bodies lying on the ground, then rode in the direction in which the woman had been so desperately searching for her children.

He quickly found tracks. At least four horses. Shod horses, White Man's horses, although the Indians around here had few horses anyhow.

He rode fast enough to cover ground, but not so fast that he would tire his horse before he reached the men he was following. They were not moving fast at all. They appeared to be very confident, probably well-armed, and feeling as if they owned this land.

He caught sight of them half an hour later, riding about a quarter mile ahead of him. Gabe immediately guided his horse into thicker cover, then studied the terrain ahead, a small valley. In the center of the valley the forest thinned out into meadow and swamp. The four horsemen seemed headed in that direction.

Taking a chance that he was right, that the men would ride through the open meadows, Gabe now began to push his horse harder, taking it around in a loop to the right, keeping a section of forest between himself and the horsemen. Within half an hour he was almost even with them, off to their right.

He stopped his horse and took out a pair of binoculars, one of the more useful of the White Man's inventions. He studied the horsemen. There were not four riders, there were six. Four white men, with two of them each holding an Indian child in front of their saddles.

Gabe put away the binoculars, then began to close in. The soft ground muffled the sound of his horse's hooves. Within a few minutes he was only a hundred and fifty yards from the kidnappers. He stopped his horse, pulling the big Sharps rifle from its scabbard as he dismounted. He rummaged in his saddlebags and pulled out a pouch of cartridges.

He was at the edge of the forest. The kidnappers were out in the open, far from cover. Gabe sat behind a fallen log. The log was just the right height. He rested the rifle's forearm on the log. He flipped up the rear sight, moved the crossbar to the hundred-and-fifty-yard mark. He eased back the big hammer, masking the sound by holding back the trigger, then releasing it when the hammer was at full cock.

He pressed the set trigger. Now the rifle would go off at a very light touch. He settled himself over the rifle, stock against his shoulder, body totally relaxed. The kidnappers were riding along unaware of his presence. He sighted on one of the men with a child in front of him. Slowly, carefully, he put pressure on the trigger, hardly breathing, totally relaxed, draped over the rifle. . . .

The rifle, seeming to go off by itself, slammed the stock back against Gabe's shoulder. The huge cloud of white smoke that had mushroomed from the muzzle made it difficult for him to see the result of his shot. As it was, he had other things to do. He flipped open the rifle's breech. Smoke curled out, but by now he was already reaching into the pouch, pulling out a paper cartridge. He placed it into the breech, then pulled the loading lever back. The breechblock closed, its sharp rear end shearing off the back of the cartridge, releasing some of the powder. It took only a second more to fit another percussion cap onto the nipple.

Now he could see better. The man he had aimed at had disappeared. The man's horse stamped nervously in a circle, with the child still on its back. The three remaining white men, obviously stunned by what had happened, were staring in Gabe's direction. In another moment they would react.

Gabe cocked the rifle, aimed again, shot a little more quickly this time, once again at a man with a child before him. Tricky shooting; he must not hit the child. This time he saw his target plucked out of the saddle as if by a giant hand. The child fell, too, but Gabe figured the man had pulled him down as he fell.

Enough with the Sharps. Gabe leaped up onto his horse, thrust the smoking buffalo gun back into its saddle scabbard, then, pulling out his Winchester, he let out a high, ululating yell and charged the two remaining white men.

One pulled out a pistol and headed straight for Gabe. The other, sensing death pounding toward him, pulled his horse's head around and spurred the startled animal into a full run . . . in the other direction.

Gabe stood in his stirrups, working the Winchester's loading lever as he opened fire on the man charging him. The man fired twice with his pistol, then, looking behind him, toward his fleeing partner, he realized he was alone. He started to turn his horse.

Too late. Gabe was on him now. Remembering the murdered man and wife, Gabe had no mercy. One of his shots hit the man in the shoulder. The man dropped his pistol, reeling in the saddle. Gabe rode right up to him. "No!" the man screamed when Gabe pointed the Winchester at him, one-handed. "For God's sake! Don't shoot!"

A coward. A man without dignity. A man who could kill an unarmed man and woman, kidnap their children, then beg for mercy. Yes, a coward. Gabe had been brought up to despise cowards, a species lower than the lowest animal. In Lakota society, a coward was a danger to the entire tribe.

Gabe shot the man in the head from less than a yard away. The man toppled off his horse, dead before he hit the ground. Gabe turned away, scanned the area. Both children were on the ground now, huddled together. Gabe ignored them for the moment, riding his horse toward the other two fallen white men. One of them was still alive. Gabe shot him through the chest. He wished there were more of the kidnappers for him to shoot, he was filled with a cold killing anger.

He debated going after the man who'd raced away. But there were the children to consider. They were still huddled together, a girl and a boy, perhaps seven and nine years old. They watched with huge eyes as Gabe rode toward them. To make them feel more at ease, he put away his rifle, then dismounted. "I will not harm you," he told them, in the same language in which he'd spoken to their dead mother.

Still, they huddled together. Gabe walked right up to them. The boy, slightly older, let go of his sister and straightened up. He was obviously still very frightened, but determined to meet Gabe with dignity. Which was the way a child of warriors should behave. "Put your sister on one of the horses," Gabe said gently. "I will take you back to your people."

The boy finally spoke. "My mother," he said, pointing back in the direction from which Gabe had come. "My father. . . ."

"First," Gabe said, just as gently as before, "we will go to your village."

The boy, realizing what Gabe's words meant, blanched. But he immediately regained control of himself. "We will go with you," he murmured. "Come, sister."

He helped the girl up onto one of the horses. She did not seem to totally realize what had happened. She mounted, her face numb with shock. The boy sprang up behind her, his arm around her waist to steady her.

The boy guided the way back to his village. It was several miles further along the valley. When the village came into sight, Gabe saw people look up, alarmed, then they ran toward their plank houses. Men came out of the doorways armed. Only one had a gun.

Then the people saw the boy and girl, and saw also that Gabe's weapons were holstered. A woman broke away from a group, ran toward the boy and girl as they rode into the center of the village. The girl half-fell from the horse into the woman's arms.

Gabe dismounted. His command of their language was still somewhat shaky, but he quickly told them what had happened. Rage and dismay contorted the features of the villagers when they heard of the deaths of the children's parents. Their anger mixed with exultation when they heard that three of the kidnappers were also dead. The men looked at Gabe with great respect. They had already heard of the strange warrior living with their cousins. Now they knew that what they had heard about him was true.

Gabe did not stay in the village for long. Three of the men went with him to collect the bodies of their slain fellow villagers. They took the horse the children had used. Both the man and the woman were carefully loaded onto the animal's back, which it did not like in the least. "Do not keep the horse," Gabe warned them. "It will only bring you trouble."

He did not ride back to the village with them. He was anxious to return to Spotted Fawn's village. If white men were out marauding, he wanted to be there to protect his woman.

On the way back to the village he realized that the boredom that had been overwhelming him for the past few weeks had completely vanished. Today he had fought. He had done a warrior's work, protecting the helpless. He felt like a man again, like a hunter. Not like a fisherman, or a pounder of acorns.

Yes, today he had done a man's work. "Aaaiiyyaaaa!" he called out softly, to the wind, to the sky, to the land.

CHAPTER EIGHTEEN

While Gabe was returning to the village, the lone survivor among the kidnappers was still racing his horse toward what he hoped was safety. He knew that his comrades were dead. He had known from the moment he saw that half-naked figure on the big black stallion come charging out of the trees that the only possibility of survival lay in flight.

Only now that the danger seemed behind him did he find time to think about what had happened. It was damned strange that one of the local Indians had attacked on horseback, charging without apparent fear. The kidnapper, whose name was Chris, had spent time out on the Plains. Out there, he'd seen Indians charge the way that Indian had charged today.

Initially, Chris's only desire had been to ride straight away from the Indian. Now, with no apparent pursuit evident, he began to angle toward the east. Toward company. Even though no one seemed to be on his trail, that damned Indian could be shadowing him, waiting to blast him out of the saddle.

An hour later Chris sighted his objective, a scattering of dilapidated cabins straggling up a ruined, logged-out slope. At first he thought no one was there, which was not good. He wanted white men around him, men with guns, in case that damned wild Indian showed up again.

A sagging door opened. A worn-looking woman wearing a torn, dirty dress started to walk outside, saw Chris, then called back into the cabin. A moment later a man came out into the open, pushing the woman out of the way. He was carrying an old Civil War style musket. An incredible tangle of black, matted hair and beard made it difficult for Chris to make out who the man was at first. Then he recognized the close-set, piggish little eyes and the man's massive frame. "Jack!" he called out, pulling his lathered horse to a slithering stop a few yards from the cabin door. "God, am I glad to see a white man!"

Jack eyed the lathered horse, noticed Chris's excited manner. "What the hell happened to you?" he asked, his voice a deep bass rumble.

"Injuns!" Chris shouted. "Opened up on us a few miles from here. Killed Slim and Bill and Henry."

Jack's mouth fell open, showing a pink gash and a few rotted teeth in the midst of all that hair. "What?" he bellowed. "Hell, there ain't been no Injun trouble round these parts for months."

By now all the excitement and yelling had brought other men out of their cabins, about half a dozen altogether, most of them lean, dirty, poor-looking men. But all of them were armed. Two more women appeared, as exhausted and worn-looking as Jack's woman. This collection of cabins was an outpost, inhabited by about a dozen men looking for gold, panning the river that lay a quarter of a mile away. Earlier, men had built shacks right next to the river; then the river had risen during a particularly bad storm and washed the shacks away. Washed away a couple of miners, too.

Chris now had a much larger audience. Dismounting, accepting a belt of home brew corn squeezings, he settled himself onto a log and began to tell his story. Which, of course, bore little similarity to what had actually happened. "They jumped us in that little valley a few miles over," he said, looking longingly at the stone jug, but it was now passing in the opposite direction, wetting gizzards other than his own. "They opened up on us from ambush," he said. "Got Slim and Bill right away."

"How many?" a man asked.

"Oh, hell. Coulda been a dozen o' the bastards. After they shot down Slim and Bill, they come ridin' outta the trees hell-for-leather, a'shootin' and a'hollerin' like a pack o' screamin' devils."

"Ridin'?" a man asked, obviously surprised.

Taken aback for a moment, but just for a moment, Chris continued. "Sure. A'ridin' like hell straight for us. Me an' Henry, we pulled out our guns an' started blastin' away, but they got Henry right away. I'd swung around wide, tryin' to get at 'em from the side, but when I saw Henry go down, an' those red devils swarm over him, I knew I'd never make it, one man 'gainst all those redskins, so I fired a coupla more shots—I think I hit one of 'em—then lit out like my horse's tail was on fire."

"You outrun 'em?" a man asked. Chris thought he could detect just a touch of disbelief in the man's voice. The poor quality of Chris's horse was well-known. Then it occurred to him that he had not actually fired his pistol at all. But what did that matter? Since he never cleaned the damned thing, it always smelled like burnt powder.

"Don't guess I woulda made it outta there," he said somberly. "But those devils, seein' three men down, swarmed all over 'em, just like I said. They was so hair-happy they didn't pay me no mind. Hell, I was in the trees by then, anyhow."

The image Chris had painted of a horde of naked savages swarming over dead or wounded white men, hacking away at their scalps, did a fine job of inflaming the men listening. "Goddamn," one man bellowed. "We cain't let them get away with it! If they kin attack four white men like that, then they'll start thinkin' 'bout hittin' us."

Most of the other men chorused their agreement. "Must be the bunch livin' further up that valley," one said. "Left the reservation a few months ago."

"They've never given anybody any trouble before," Jack said, scratching his beard thoughtfully. He looked straight at Chris, wondering if there was more to this story. Or maybe even less.

Chris, by now basking in a lot of attention, did not notice. Of course, he had said nothing at all about kidnapping the Indian brats, or about the way Slim and Bill had gunned down their parents. That had been a damned shame. The woman had been pretty good-looking. If Slim had been a little more patient about getting that knife away from her . . . But she'd cut him on the arm, and he'd put one right between those nice little tits.

Uh-uh. No point in saying anything about the kidnapping. Or about anything else. By now, Chris was beginning to believe his own story. There had been a lot of shooting coming from the trees, enough to blow Slim and Bill right out of their saddles. Chris's untidy, lazy, rather simple mind had little trouble conjuring up an image of at least half a dozen bloodthirsty Indian bucks riding right behind the big one who'd shot down Henry.

The little settlement was now humming like a disturbed wasps' nest. Several men were shouting at once, but the general drift was clear. They wanted revenge. One of the women murmured something to her man, about not stirring up any more trouble with the Indians. He casually back-handed her across her already bruised face, as unaware of doing it as if he'd absentmindedly brushed away an annoying mosquito. Humboldt County's women did not have a much easier life than the Indian women.

Within half an hour, plans were being made to attack the village. As usual, Jack took charge. "I figure there ain't more'n a coupla dozen Injuns there," he told the others. "If we hit 'em by surprise, they won't have a chance to fight back."

Other men nodded. Of course, the available supply of Indians in the village far outstripped Chris's image of a horde of mounted attackers. The men all knew Chris, knew that he tended to exaggerate. Probably four, five Indians at the most had bushwhacked Chris and the others. Chris's imagination had furnished the other attackers. Not that they held it against him. What mattered was that white men had been killed by Indians. That was a wrong that had to be righted. If the Indians started getting the idea that they could kill white men at will, things could get out of hand. There were men here who remembered the Indian wars of a decade before, which had made this county a dangerous place for whites . . . until the army had been called in to teach the Indians a lesson. Well, there were enough good men here to teach that outlaw village a lesson they'd never forget.

By early afternoon, more men had come up from the river, until a dozen were ready to ride, all of them heavily armed. They did not have quite enough horses, but with a couple of men riding double behind others, they finally got under way.

Jack took charge, had taken charge from the first. His size, general meanness, and the fact that he was marginally smarter than the others gave him a natural authority over this bunch of ignorant, drunken misfits. Not that it was all that easy to exercise that authority. Totally undisciplined, the men rode noisily, loudly bragging to one another how many Indians they were going to kill, doing their best to quiet their own nervousness. Most of the men, half-believing Chris's story, were beginning to wonder if it was a good idea to tackle a passel of Indians who had already wiped out a party of three white men.

Jack was aware that several of the men were drinking, passing stone jugs of white lightning from hand to hand. That he would let pass, also. The alcohol would bolster their courage.

Jack had fought in the War. He'd been a corporal in a company of Confederate border raiders, Texans, mostly. They'd killed, raped, and robbed their way across parts of Kansas and Missouri. Jack had liked the War, liked the feeling of power it gave him, the sense that he could do anything to other people that he wanted to do, without the law coming after him. Indians were his target now. Legally, they were helpless.

In the late afternoon they reached the place where Gabe had killed the three kidnappers. The men rode up to the bodies and sat their horses, looking down at the dead men. Crows, or other scavengers, had pecked out the eyes of one of the men, but otherwise, the bodies were not mutilated. Jack turned toward Chris. "Thought you said the Injuns took their hair," he said.

Chris shrugged, looked away. "I said they was a'swarmin' all over 'em," he replied.

Jack rode around the area. Then he rode back to face Chris. "Don't see many hoofprints neither. Should be more, if they charged out of those trees. How many did you say there were?"

Chris was by now looking very uncomfortable. "Well, Gawd, Jack, I wasn't a'countin'."

Yeah . . . just running, Jack thought. He stared hard at Chris, but said nothing more. As far as he could see, there had probably been no more than one or two attackers. Well, what difference did it make? White men had been killed. Blood demanded blood. And the very fact that the attackers had been few suggested that there was not a great deal of danger in hitting the Indians. "Come on, boys," Jack said. "Let's go get the bastards!"

A clear line of hoofprints led away from the site of the killings. Two horses. Jack saw at once that one of the horses was shod. Probably one of the dead men's horses. Jack wondered why all three horses hadn't been taken. Who cared? All that mattered was that there was going to be a lot of fun ahead.

It was less than an hour before dark when they saw smoke rising ahead, in several thin columns. "Cooking fires," Jack grunted to the others. "Must be the village."

The skylarking and drinking that had earlier marked the men's behavior had by now completely fallen away. Fighting lay ahead. The thought of potential danger affected each of the men differently. Some were swallowing nervously, others grinned a wolfish grin. Some had no expression at all on their faces.

"Fan out," Jack said. "We'll go straight in, at a walk at first, then, when I give the signal, ride like hell."

He kicked his horse into a fast walk. After a moment's hesitation, other men did the same. Jack glanced to the sides. As he'd expected, the men were not fanning out enough. It would be better if they fanned out in a circle, completely surrounding the village, but he doubted he could get enough of these assholes to leave the security of the pack. He'd have to take them in just as they were.

He hoped they'd be able to surprise the Indians, who had at least one good fighter amongst them, the man, or men, who'd shot the hell out of Chris's group. So there might be a strong fight. Good. Jack had not felt this alive since his last raid. Damn, that was almost eight years ago. He and the company had attacked a small town in Kansas known for its Northern sympathies. They'd surprised the town, it had been a Sunday, and most of the people were in church. It had been a wild time. Jack had killed six men. And then . . . there'd been the women. Women were always the best part of a raid. God, how some of them had screamed!

The village was in sight now, just a few smallish plank houses. There couldn't be many people there. Probably not many more than the dozen Jack had. And many of the villagers would be women and children. Maybe it'd be too easy a fight.

They were sighted when they were about a hundred yards away. An old man looked up, stared vaguely into the distance, then, when his old eyes finally figured out what all that movement meant, he let out a wild shout of alarm.

"That cuts it, boys!" Jack shouted. "Let's git 'em!"

Spurs raked flanks. Jack, riding a little ahead of the others, let out a Texas yell. He liked that yell, loved the sound of it. Texans knew what to do with dirty Indians, and Mexicans, and any other human trash that might get in their way.

The old man had run into a house. He ran back out now, fitting an arrow to a bowstring. Jack shot him through the stomach. Other men were running out of houses now; the villagers had been in the middle of eating their evening meal. There were very few men; Jack could count only four, besides the old man.

One of the Indians had a gun. An old musket. He raised it and fired. A man behind Jack let out a howl of pain as a bullet grazed his shoulder. Half a dozen guns roared, and the Indian with the musket fell dead, hit three times.

Now, the fight turned into a simple hunt, an extermination. The remaining three Indian men were quickly killed. Which left only the women and children, and two of the children were already down, one little girl with her head blown apart. The raiders leaped from their horses, began chasing the screaming women.

One woman had her arms around two children, a boy and a girl, each about five years old. A real looker, Jack thought. Nice and young. Good tits. He walked up to the woman. She was backing away, dragging the children with her. He could see that she was trying to get close to the woods, then maybe she'd try and fight him, slow him down, while the children ran for the cover of the trees.

Damned if he'd let any of them get away. He leaned his rifle against the side of a house, then pulled his pistol and shot the children before the woman could get in front of them. The screams of the dying children, the blood spurting from their bodies, froze the woman in place long enough for Jack to leap forward and club her to the ground with the barrel of his pistol.

She lay on her back, her head bloody. She was too groggy from the blow to resist when Jack tore her skirt off. He was on her quickly, pulling his pants down. He loved the look of pain and horror on her face. God, he felt good! Rape was the only way an honest man could let goddamn females know who was really boss. He thought sourly of the thin, worn-out body of his own woman. Not much to look at, compared to this Indian girl.

After he was finished with her, he reached for his knife and cut the girl's throat. Damned if he'd let anyone else have a woman that he'd had. The girl was still thrashing on the ground, spouting blood, when Jack turned away, buttoning his trousers. Most of the Indians were dead by now, or close to it. He saw Chris on top of a woman, his pants down around his knees, pounding away. "Goddamn, Chris," one of the other men said. "How the hell kin you do that? Half her head's blowed away. She's dead as a hammer."

Chris laughed, a high-pitched cackle. "So what?" he yelped. "She's still warm."

Jack walked through the village, examining the bodies. A boy of seven or eight lay dead above the body of a girl a year or two younger. As if he'd been protecting her. The boy held a knife in his hand. There was a smear of blood on the blade. Damned if the little bastard hadn't fought back.

Funny. None of the dead Indians looked like the kind of warrior who'd be able to take on four armed white men and leave three of them dead. Jack was beginning to wonder if this village had even been involved.

Ah, what the hell? Indians were Indians, and blood debts had to be paid. He looked around the village again, at the twisted bodies, listened to the screams of the one woman still alive. Smoke was already rising from some of the houses, which his men were starting to burn.

His men. Just like in the old days. Yeah, he thought, looking around him once more. Days like this, really exciting days, were few and far between.

CHAPTER NINETEEN

Late the next morning a survivor of the massacre staggered into Spotted Fawn's village. She was a woman of about thirty, who had been picking berries in the forest when the white men attacked. She had traveled all night, until fatigue and fear had forced her to stop. She'd hidden in a thicket for hours, certain that the white men would find her and kill her as they had killed the others.

At dawn, she continued on. She knew where she was going; she had a sister in Spotted Fawn's village. She finally arrived, exhausted, scratched and bloody from running through brambles the night before. During the massacre it had been the berry patch that had saved her. She'd burrowed deep in among the thorns, able to see most of what happened, but well-hidden.

Once in her sister's village, she was first made to sit down and drink some water. Her sister wanted her to eat some soup, but the woman could not stop herself from talking. She had to tell what she'd seen, cleanse the horror of it from her mind by putting it into words. "They came while most of the people were getting ready to eat," she said to the circle of horrified people surrounding her. "That was why I was picking berries . . . for the meal. They came riding horses, rode into the village and began killing. All except for some of the women, whom they . . . killed later."

Gabe stood at the back of the circle, wooden-faced, saying nothing. As the woman described the horrors she'd watched, the systematic butchery, the rapes, and finally, the burning of the houses, he had no doubt why it had happened. It had been his fault. The massacre was in revenge for the men he'd killed, the ones who'd kidnapped the children. There might not have been any further trouble, but he'd let the fourth man get away. He'd survived to tell his tale to other white men. A tale that probably told of an attack by an Indian . . . because Gabe had been dressed as an Indian, had given his war cry as he charged. When bullets were flying and bodies falling, a frightened man—and that surviving kidnapper had fled like a coward—was not likely to notice that his attacker had light-colored hair and gray eyes. No. All that man would remember was an Indian in a breechclout, shooting down the men he was with.

That was Gabe's mistake; he'd let that coward live to tell the tale, to talk about it to other white men. Who would want revenge. Not out of some noble sentiment—he'd seen little that was noble in Humboldt County—but out of fear. The White Man in Humboldt was an intruder, and he rightly feared the people whose land he was stealing. Any reaction would naturally be brutal.

Gabe walked away from where the woman, who was half-insane with grief, was telling her story, reciting horror after horror. He went inside Spotted Fawn's house, where most of his gear was, then immediately began to put on his white man's clothing. Spotted Fawn had seen him leave the others. She followed and entered the house just as he was strapping on his shoulder holster. "You are going," she said, rather than asked.

"I have to," he replied.

She looked down at the ground, trying to hide her fear. "That woman . . . she says that there were many white men."

"I know. But they must pay. They cannot be permitted to get away with this. They might strike here next."

There was a short silence as he pulled on his linen duster and adjusted it over the shoulder holster.

"You blame yourself," Spotted Fawn finally said.

He nodded. "Yes. I was arrogant. Too sure of myself. I brought this thing to their village."

She looked down at the ground again. "Perhaps," she said hesitantly, "the most dangerous kind of arrogance is to blame yourself for that which you could not help. Could you really have let those men take away the children?"

He moved closer to Spotted Fawn, raised her chin with his right hand, looked into her dark, troubled eyes. "No. Perhaps not. But still, those men must not survive."

She shook her head sorrowfully. "Then other white men will want revenge."

"But not against you."

He pointed to his hat, his trousers, his linen duster. "I will go as a white man. If they want revenge against other white men, they are welcome to it."

"And if you die?" she asked quietly, looking up at his face, her own face grave.

"Then I die. As a warrior."

Spotted Fawn struggled with herself for a moment. Her mother had been killed, her father, her whole family. Was she now about to lose this man who had come into her life, who had, in fact, practically re-created her life? But what could she say, without insulting him? He was right. A warrior was a warrior and must act as a warrior. Especially this man . . . or he would be less than the man he was. "Do not die," she said simply. "Kill them, then come back."

Gabe gently stroked the girl's cheek, then pulled her close against him. For just a moment her arms went around his waist, then they both stepped back. One last, lingering look, then Gabe stepped outside.

He was saddling his horse when Salmon noticed what he was doing, how he was dressed. Salmon and his lodge mates came up to Gabe. "You are going after them," Salmon said, as flatly as Spotted Fawn had spoken.

Gabe nodded. Salmon took him by the arm. "Wait. We will go with you. I had friends, and some others here had relatives in that village."

Gabe shook his head. "I will go alone. I will have to ride fast. Men on foot would fall behind."

"No!" Salmon said explosively. "You forget that now I have a horse. And a rifle that cries out for blood."

Gabe turned to face his friend. "Then blood will come to this place. The same thing will happen here, as at that other village. You know how it is in this land; you would only give the white men an excuse to kill more of you. Or call in the army again. I must go alone."

Common sense began to erode Salmon's stubborn resolve. Gabe spoke quickly. "What you can do is take some men to that village. Look for any survivors. And take care of the dead."

Salmon's face was still angry, but his friends, having neither horses nor guns, took Salmon by the arms and began to reason with him. By now, Gabe was mounting his horse. As he got ready to ride away, he could see that Salmon had been convinced that he must not go. But he did not like it. "It is a terrible thing," he called out after Gabe, "when a man cannot avenge his own people!"

Gabe rode away without looking back. He was afraid that he would see Spotted Fawn, that his resolve would weaken. How much easier it would be to stay here in the village and hope that no trouble came this way. To stay and fight only for those he knew so well.

But a great wrong had been done. And his own carelessness had contributed to that wrong. He should have gone after that fourth kidnapper, killed him before he could tell his tale. But he had not been able to leave the two frightened children. Perhaps he had been right in doing that, but now it was those children, and their entire village, who had paid for his lack of ruthlessness.

He reached the village in the early afternoon. He was still a quarter of a mile away when he smelled the smoke. He rode wide around the village, looking for ambushes. Then, as he got close enough to see into the smoking, ruined place, he became aware of the boldness of the vultures. They were all over the bodies, which told Gabe that he would find no one there but the dead.

He rode straight in. The vultures immediately took alarm, but many were too bloated with carrion to fly away. He loosened his lariat, snapped it at the remaining birds, who waddled behind bushes. A careful examination of the area failed to find any survivors. Gabe rode to the edge of the forest, called out in the local language, but no one answered, no one came out of the trees. Apparently the woman who had made it to Spotted Fawn's village was the only survivor.

A few minutes later he found the boy and girl he'd rescued from the kidnappers. The vultures had not yet paid them much attention, so they were recognizable. He saw how the boy's body lay protecting the girl, saw the dried, dark blood on his pitiful little knife, knew that the boy had fought for his sister's life. In vain.

As Gabe rode around the village, looking for tracks, he felt a cold deadness inside himself. What he had just seen had become far too familiar a part of his life. Massacred villages. The bodies of those who had lost their lives to a more powerful, more ruthless people. And not all of the massacres he'd seen had been committed by white men. The Red Man was just as capable of savagery . . . although far less efficient at extermination than the White Man, who had a vision of an entire continent to conquer. Who had a plan.

Blood must be paid for with blood. Gabe followed the tracks that led into, then away from the village. From the tracks, there had probably been close to a dozen men. Too many to face straight out; he'd have to use his brains.

The killers had made no attempt to conceal their tracks. Why should they? White power ruled this land, and few white men would condemn them for what they had done . . . wiping out a village of murdering, heathen savages.

Not long before dark, Gabe saw, about a quarter of a mile ahead, several crude shacks and cabins littering the side of a gentle, logged-over slope. The tracks he'd been following headed straight for the cabins. There was no great sign of life among the buildings, just a couple of men sitting in front of one of the cabins, drinking out of a jug, and a woman taking tattered garments off a sagging clothesline.

Gabe sat his horse for several minutes, studying the scene. The sun was about to set, soon it would be dark. Caution suggested a night attack, a stealthy weeding out of one man after another. Then it occurred to him that perhaps the men he was watching at the moment had had nothing to do with the massacre. Perhaps the actual killers had simply ridden through this area, and these were innocent men.

Gabe nudged his horse forward, straight toward the slope with its cabins. He was spotted while he was still a hundred yards away. The woman at the clothesline watched him for a few seconds, then walked quickly toward a doorway, looked inside, then called out something.

Gabe was only a short distance away when a man came out of the cabin. The man said something to the woman, then stood watching Gabe warily. He was a big man, with a thick tangle of matted black hair and beard hiding most of his features. Gabe stopped his horse five yards away from the man, who, so far, had said nothing. Nor had Gabe.

The two men with the jug came over. One of them, obviously a little drunk, grinned up at Gabe, and said, "Howdy, stranger. What parts you be comin' from?"

"East of here," Gabe replied. He carefully scanned the entire area, although he was careful to conceal his interest.

"Ridin' on through?" the big man with all the hair around his face asked, his voice deep and rough.

"Toward the coast."

Gabe looked around more openly now. "Quite a little settlement you've got here. Farming? Ranching?"

"Hell no," one of the men with the jug said. "We're prospectors." He laughed, a short, bitter bark. "Lookin' for El Dorado."

The other jug man laughed more noisily. The man with all the hair did not laugh, just kept studying Gabe. By now a couple of other men had come out of their cabins and were drifting toward Gabe and the others. Gabe was wondering what to say next, when he saw something hanging under the eaves of a cabin, the one the man with the hair had come out of. Long, dark, matted objects. "Are those what

I think they are?" he asked no one in particular, pointing.

One of the drinkers snorted with laughter. "Yep. Scalps."

"Shut up, Pete," the hairy man rumbled.

The drinker looked offended. "Ah hell, Jack," he replied. "I got just as much right to say what . . ."

But, at a scowl from the man he'd called Jack, his voice died away. Gabe ignored them all, rode closer to the scalps. Back at the massacred village he'd noticed that several of the bodies had been scalped. He had obviously come to the right place. "They look like Indian scalps," he said.

One of the drinkers giggled. "Hell yes. You think we'd go around scalpin' white men?"

There were now half a dozen men gathering close. Gabe swept his eyes over them. They were a rancid-looking bunch. Some appeared to be nervous as Gabe reached out to touch one of the hanging scalps, gave it a gentle push that started it swaying. "I passed an Indian village further east," he said, his voice expressionless. "Nothing there but bodies. Everyone wiped out. Looked like they got taken completely by surprise."

Perhaps it was the uninterested sound of his voice, or perhaps Jack simply wanted to brag, to share his triumph with someone beside the slobs who daily surrounded him. "That was us," he said, with a touch of pride. "Murdering savages killed some of our friends. We paid 'em back."

Gabe rode back toward Jack. "I think I heard something about that," he said, his voice a little less disinterested now. "About the white men who were killed."

"Oh yeah?" Jack asked, suddenly more cautious.

Gabe nodded. "I heard they kidnapped some Indian children. Killed their parents."

Jack's eyes narrowed. That damned Chris, he thought. He never told me. I shoulda asked.

He scowled and said aloud, "What the hell difference does it make? They killed white men. That means they hadda die, we hadda make an example out of 'em."

"That's right," one of the other men called out. "What the hell do a few Indian brats matter, anyhow? The sooner we wipe 'em all out, the less we'll hafta worry about 'em sneakin' up on us."

Sitting his horse, unmoving, Gabe said softly, "Well . . . I suppose those Indian brats only mattered to the Indians themselves."

The men standing around him were beginning to grow restless, even a little angry. "What the hell are you?" a man called out. "Some kinda Injun lover?"

"A whole village," Gabe said just as softly. "Wiped out."

"Maybe you oughta go live with the Indians, mister, you love 'em so much."

Gabe was already guiding his horse through the men. There were far too many to fight, surrounded as he was. Angry faces were turned up toward him. Some of the men wore pistols. He suspected that at least a portion of their anger toward him came from a vague sense of guilt, augmented by fear that they might somehow have to pay for what they'd done. That kind of fear could turn into sudden, deadly rage.

Gabe's horse broke through the men. "They killed white men," a voice called after him. "They hadda be taught a lesson."

Gabe was twenty yards away, heading for the edge of the woods, where the trees came closest to the cabins. Only another thirty yards to go. He turned in the saddle without stopping his horse. "*They* didn't kill the white men," he said, loudly enough for all the men to hear. "Someone else did."

He had almost reached the edge of the forest when another man came out of a cabin, having been awakened from a drunken nap by all the shouting. The cabin he came out of was close to the woods. Gabe rode right by him. The man looked up at the big man on the tall black horse. He had several seconds to look into his face, to notice the pale eyes, the long sandy hair.

The man was Chris. Still half-asleep, he was aware of his mind working away at something, probing a fuzzy memory. Then, just as the horseman disappeared into the trees, the memory coalesced. A moment later he was running toward the men grouped around Jack's cabin. "Goddamn!" he shouted. "That's him!"

Jack's mind was still working on what the stranger had said. How the hell had he known so much about those Indians? He'd said that they hadn't killed Slim and Bill and Henry. That someone else had killed them. But how could he know that, unless . . . ?

Chris's yelling broke his concentration. "That's who?" Jack demanded.

Chris stopped not three feet away, his face wild, his right arm pointing toward the spot in the trees where the rider had disappeared. "That's him!" Chris repeated. "That's the bastard that killed Slim and Bill and Henry!"

"Whatta you mean?" Jack roared. "You said it was a buncha Injuns! That ain't no Injun!"

But the stranger had known about the killings. And, in a way, he kind of looked like an Indian. Jack felt a cold chill settle over him. The bastard had been sitting his horse just a few feet away!

While Jack wrestled with possibilities, Gabe took advantage of the confusion between Chris and Jack to ride to his left through the forest until he reached the highest point on the slope, From there, some of the cabins screened him from the men below. He slipped his Winchester from its scabbard, cocked the hammer, then rode out into the open.

He rode most of the way unseen. He was only about forty yards from the excited, arguing men before they spotted him. "Jesus Christ!" someone screamed. "He's back!"

Letting the reins drop, kicking his horse into a gallop, guiding the stallion with his knees, Gabe charged straight at the men, firing the Winchester into their packed mass, working the loading lever rapidly. Two men fell before the startled men began to scatter, before they began reaching for their weapons.

At the last moment, Gabe veered off to the right, sweeping past the running men, shooting down three more. Shots were beginning to come his way. Wild shots. He swerved his horse behind a cabin, then raced for the nearest patch of forest. The cabin shielded him part of the way, but by now more shots were coming from the miners, some of them whistling very close.

Gabe rode in among the trees. The huge trunks easily absorbed the lead coming after him. He immediately rode to his right, then approached the forest's edge again. Dismounting, he peered around a tree.

More men, alerted by the firing, had come out of various cabins. He could hear some of them shouting, asking what the hell was going on. Men were running every which way, most of them staring at the point in the forest wall where Gabe had disappeared.

He slipped the Sharps out its saddle scabbard and shoved a handful of its huge cartridges into the pocket of his duster. Kneeling, he sighted on one of the men, then pulled the trigger. At this range, no more than about fifty yards, it was an easy shot. The man, hit by the huge slug, flew backward, bouncing off the side wall of one of the cabins.

Reloading quickly, Gabe shot two more of the men. There were no more targets now; the survivors had all disappeared behind cover. They were firing wildly into the woods, some of the shots clipping branches very close to Gabe. The smoke from the Sharps had given away his position.

Slipping back into the cover of the trees, he quickly mounted, then rode deeper into the forest. Riding in a big circle, he approached the forest edge again. But there was not much to see. Most of the men had retreated into the cabins. Continuing his circuit, he saw Chris crouched behind a stump, watching the point from which Gabe had last fired. Raising the Sharps, Gabe blew away half the man's head.

Fading back into the forest, Gabe tried to remember how many men he'd shot. Eight, possibly as many as nine. There couldn't be many of them left. But the survivors would be well-fortified by now, jumpy, ready to shoot at the first sign of movement.

Gabe rode to the far side of the hill. Finding a hidden spot, he staked his horse out on a long line, so that it could feed. Then, taking his Winchester, he slipped back through the trees, toward the cabins.

It was almost completely dark. Gabe used the last few minutes of light to study the cabins and the ground around them. A lot of stumps had been left, and the area was littered with debris. There was good cover most of the way to the cabins.

Gabe settled down to wait. He was good at waiting, had spent a great deal of time when he'd been with the Oglala waiting patiently, laying out ambushes, remaining motionless with his fellow warriors until the enemy was certain no one could be near.

For two hours he waited. He could hear a little calling back and forth between two of the cabins. That seemed to be where the miners had holed up, in two cabins about twenty yards apart. Listening patiently, Gabe came to the conclusion that there were no more than three or four of the men still in condition to fight.

The voices began to grow cranky. "Hell . . . he's lit out," one man said loudly enough for Gabe to hear. Another voice told him to shut up, that he'd give them away. Gabe recognized that last voice . . . it was the man called Jack.

He'd had time to think about Jack. Behind all that hair, he'd noticed a pair of bright, appraising eyes. The eyes were cruel, with perhaps a touch of madness, but shrewd. Jack was obviously the man he would have to worry about. The most intelligent among a scurvy crew.

Now Gabe knew where Jack was . . . back in the cabin he'd originally come out of. Gabe, moving silently on his belly, taking advantage of every bit of cover, of every inky shadow, began to work his way toward that cabin. It took him nearly an hour to reach it, but finally he was in position, not far from the door.

This close, he could hear better. Whispers were coming from inside the cabin. There were two people, one of them probably a woman. Then Gabe heard Jack's voice, coming from a side window, calling out softly to the other cabin. "I'm goin' outside, boys. If that bastard's anywhere near, I'm gonna find him."

A mutter of agreement from the other cabin. Then soft footsteps padding toward the door. Gabe melted into the shadow of the stump behind which he was crouched. A moment later the door opened, onto a rectangle of darkness. Slight movement, as Jack poked one eye around the corner of the door frame. Then a quicker movement as Jack ducked through the doorway and dodged into the shadow of a stump.

Gabe's stump. Except that he and Jack were on opposite sides.

Jack called toward the other cabin again, barely above a whisper, but the sound carried well in the quiet night air. "I'm heading off to the right. A coupla you assholes go the other way."

"Hell no," the answer came back, far too loudly. "We oughta stay holed up nice an' safe until it's light, then do our lookin'."

"Ah, you lousy, gutless . . ."

Jack slowly stood up, then began to edge around the stump, which had been cut off about four feet above the ground. He did not see the dark shadow on the stump's far side until it was nearly at his feet. "What the hell?" he blurted out.

By then it was too late. Gabe rose smoothly to his feet, his knife in his right hand. Pushing aside Jack's rifle with his left hand, he drove the knife deep into Jack's belly. Staggering backward, Jack let out a wild cry, a roar of pain and surprise. Still holding onto the rifle, which Jack was trying to twist toward him, Gabe followed. The knife went in one, two, three more times, the last thrust straight into Jack's heart. Jack's grip loosened on the rifle, and he fell backward, slowly, almost gracefully. "Oh, God," Gabe heard him gasp one last time.

The men in the other cabin had heard Jack's death cry. "What the hell's goin' on out there?" one shouted.

Nothing. Silence. A long, dread silence, as Gabe, picking up his Winchester, zigzagged toward the second cabin. He heard one of the men inside say, "It hadda be Jack. The son of a bitch got Jack."

"Oh, God."

Gabe, about ten feet from the cabin, called out, "You in there. You know why you have to die."

Silence from inside the cabin. They would never come out now. Gabe wondered if he should set fire to the cabin, but he did not know where he might find kerosene. He did not like the idea of going into any of the other cabins to look. Most of the men must be dead, but there'd been women, too. They could gun him down as surely as any of the men. And he did not want to put himself in the position of having to kill the women.

He quietly ran up to the cabin and flattened himself against its front wall, within a couple of feet of the door. The wall was made of logs, the men inside would never be able to fire through the logs. But the door was flimsy. Reaching out, Gabe smashed the butt of his rifle against the door's splintery, warped boards, then quickly pulled back. Almost immediately, a barrage of shots came through the door, near the point where he'd struck it. Gabe let out a terrible yell, as if he'd been hit.

Silence from inside, then, a moment later, a voice saying hopefully, "I think we done it, Fred. I think we got the bastard."

"Well, hell," a sour voice came back. "You go out an' see. I ain't a'movin' from this here cabin."

Only two men then, and now the sound of their voices had given away their positions . . . close to the door. Gabe stepped right in front of the partially splintered door, leveled his rifle, and blasted a dozen quick shots inside. The shots almost drowned out the screams as the men were hit, but, once he'd finished shooting, the awful silence from inside the cabin suggested to Gabe that he'd killed both of them.

Gabe stood up, although he still kept close to cover. He heard whimpering coming from one of the cabins. A woman's whimpering. "You women!" he called out. "I have no war with you. Your men committed a crime. They've been punished. That's enough for now. But I want you to remember one thing. When you see other white men, tell them what has happened here. Tell them that any who attack or harass the Indian people to whom this land belongs will suffer the same fate."

He'd said too much, pinpointed his position. Gabe immediately slipped to the side, in case any wounded survivors opened up on him. There! Something moving by Jack's cabin! A flare of light. Someone was lighting a lantern. Gabe raised his rifle. Then, in the dim lantern light, he saw that it was a woman. The woman who had gone in to warn Jack when Gabe had first ridden up to the cabins.

Apparently she was not afraid of being shot. Or perhaps she simply didn't care. Gabe watched her search the area with a lantern until she'd located Jack's body. She stood over the body for a good thirty seconds, looking down, not moving. Then, as Gabe started to slip away, back toward the cover of the forest, he heard the woman's voice, a low, tired voice, a voice without emotion.

From where he was standing, Gabe could barely make out the words. "God, I'm glad you're dead, you son of a bitch," the woman said to the half-gutted corpse lying at her feet.

CHAPTER TWENTY

When Gabe returned to the village, the only answer he gave to Salmon's questions was, "They are dead. All of them are dead."

After unsaddling his horse, he went straight to Spotted Fawn's house. She knew he had arrived, but, as if already aware of his mood, she had remained in the house, waiting.

Wordlessly, she helped Gabe off with his duster and shoulder holster. He left on his trousers and shirt; it was chilly. He sat by the central fire pit, staring into the flames.

"It is over, then?" Spotted Fawn finally asked.

Gabe shook his head. "No. What I did, the deaths of the men I killed today, was only justice. It was not victory. The white men will come again. They will keep coming until they have everything they want. And what they want is everything."

How could he explain to Spotted Fawn what he had seen in other places? The White Man's drive to own, to possess, to keep on going, no matter how many times he lost. "All we have gained," he muttered, as much to himself as to Spotted Fawn, "is time. And probably not very much of that."

Time. Of which the people, his or Spotted Fawn's, compared to the White Man, had a very different concept. To the White Man, time was a straight line, running from past to future, with a promise of change, of progress. For the Red

Man, past, present, and future were not clearly separated. They were all part of the same state of being. Most of the people in this village, knowing a victory had been won over the white men, would now contentedly settle down to their daily routines, as if this moment, this day, would go on forever.

Gabe had, at one time, shared that view of the world. Living among the whites had destroyed that peace of mind. Now he was aware of the future, of possibilities. In the case of the struggle against the White Man in Humboldt County, he knew the certainty of what would happen. He might continue to go out and win victories for this village, but each victory, each white man killed, only strengthened the resolve of the other whites, and there would be more and more of them coming to these forests, to fight back hard against whatever had temporarily bested them. Gabe was beginning to realize that his actions were actually a threat to this peaceful village.

Aware of days running out, Gabe moved into Spotted Fawn's house, directly against local custom. Spotted Fawn was a little uneasy at first, but soon grew contented, sharing a nightly bed with her husband.

Daytimes, Gabe put on his white man's clothing and patrolled the valley and its approaches. Still, he was surprised when Salmon came to him one day. "There is a white man living further down the valley," Salmon said. "He has built a house."

Gabe immediately saddled his horse. This time Salmon insisted on going along. Together, they rode down the valley. Salmon led him to a flimsy shack, half-propped against the bole of a giant tree. As they rode up, a white man came out of the door of the shack. The door was a simple piece of hanging deer hide. The man froze when he saw Gabe and Salmon. Gabe saw him glance quickly back through the doorway. Perhaps he had a gun inside.

"What are you doing here?" Gabe asked.

Reassured by plain English coming from the more white-looking of his two visitors, the man replied, "Jus' goin' out to take a leak."

"What are you doing on this *land?*" Gabe insisted. "This is Indian land."

The man looked genuinely surprised. "That ain't what they told me."

"Who told you?"

"Why . . . the people at the mill. Told me this was free land, open to settling. That I could file a timber claim here."

"They told you wrong," Gabe said coldly. "You will have to leave."

"Well, Gawd, mister," the man said, nervously scuffing his feet. "If I do that, Mr. Jackson ain't gonna like it at all. He already paid me."

Gabe started to pull his horse around. "If you are still here when we come back tomorrow," he told the man, "we will kill you and burn your cabin."

The man's face paled. He seemed unable to reply. Gabe and Salmon rode away, but all the way back to the village, Gabe wondered what the man had meant when he said that a Mr. Jackson had paid him. Paid him for what?

However, when he and Salmon rode back to the shack the next day, the man was gone, the shack empty. He and Salmon, using lariats, pulled down the flimsy structure. It was not difficult.

A week later, Gabe, riding down the valley, saw a thin spiral of smoke ahead. Investigating, he saw another shack. This time a white man was sitting on the ground in front of the shack, drinking from a stone jug. He made no move to get up when Gabe rode toward him. His friendly smile surprised Gabe. The man waved the jug. "Get ye down, friend," he said. "I'll share a drop with ye."

Gabe glanced around quickly, looking for hidden men whose presence might be bolstering the man's courage. He saw no one. But when he dismounted, he took his Winchester with him. The man's eyes widened a little. "This is not a robbery, I'm prayin'."

"No," Gabe said, a little confused. "But I want to know what you're doing here."

The man lifted the jug, looked at it, said, "Passin' time. Doin' my best to make the days go by." He pointed to a pile of stone jugs near the shack's doorway. "I put a good deal o' Mr. Jackson's money into liquid cheer."

That name again. Jackson. Gabe sat on the ground a few feet from the man. "Why would this Mr. Jackson give you money?"

The man appeared to be surprised by the question. "Why . . . to stay here, of course. I wouldn't stay in this dreary wilderness unless I was paid for it, now would I?"

Sitting this close, Gabe realized that the man was very drunk. Deeply drunk, in the way that a man who lives for drink can be drunk, still able to talk, to function, but with his mind floating on a sea of alcohol, rudderless.

Which was a fitting image, because, as Gabe settled down to talk to the man, he discovered that he was a sailor, beached in Humboldt County, penniless. Gabe had already noticed that the man had an accent. He was an Irish sailor. Perhaps he'd been beached because of his drinking.

The man explained the money. It was the reason for living in the shack. Like the other man Gabe and Salmon had chased away, he had filed a timber claim. Not that he had any intention of interrupting his drinking by chopping down trees. "We stay here for a while, ye see," the man, whose name was Dugan, told Gabe. "We establish a claim, under those new laws, then we sell it to Mr. Jackson."

Mr. Jackson, according to Dugan, owned one of the largest lumber companies in Humboldt County. Apparently he wanted to own an even larger company. Most of the land in this part of the county belonged to the state or to the federal government. A new law, meant to encourage settlement of the area, to split it up among many small holders, had been passed. As Dugan explained it, a man could file a timber claim. He was expected to work the claim, but a loophole in the law allowed big owners like Jackson to circumvent its intent by using men like Dugan as a front.

"He's pickin' sailors off ships," Dugan said. "Drifters. Gives us money to sit out here long enough to make the claim all nice an' legal. Then he has us sign the land over to him."

For just a moment Dugan's drunkenness lifted enough for him to take a closer look at Gabe. Not that his speech changed; he had been speaking with remarkable clearness. But something registered in his eyes. "Say," he asked. "Would ye be that man they warned us about? The half-Indian?"

"Probably."

A moment's look of alarm, but then the drunkenness swept back, deadening Dugan's sense of survival. He laughed. "Ye don't appear near as vicious as Larrabee made ye sound."

"Larrabee?" Gabe asked. He remembered the man he'd shot it out with in Eureka, the day he killed the two gunmen from the reservation. Larrabee, the assassin.

"Aye. He works for Mr. Jackson."

Dugan thought a while. "A bad-seemin' man, our Mr. Larrabee."

Gabe kept asking questions. Bit by bit he pieced it together. Jackson, the mill owner, wanted this land. He would get it by any means. By now he'd discovered that there were Indians living further up the valley. At one time it might have been easy to simply drive them away, but the warning Gabe had left with the women, after he'd killed the men who'd massacred that other village, had gotten around. This was a dangerous place to break in on. Motive was needed. And Gabe was expected to supply that motive.

"Oh, yer said to be quite a dangerous man," Dugan said amiably. "They expect ye to do somethin' violent. That's where Larrabee comes in. That'll be his excuse. He'll ride in here with fifty or a hundred men, clean out the Indians, an' have yer hide."

Dugan looked up curiously at Gabe. "Did ye do somethin' to irritate the man? Larrabee hates ye like poison."

Gabe left a few minutes later, without demanding that Dugan leave. There was little use; Jackson would only send another in his place. Besides, he doubted Dugan was in any condition to stand up, let alone walk.

On the ride back to the village, Gabe paid no attention to the sights and sounds around him. All of his concentration was internal. This was it, then. The end of the life he'd been living for the past few months. Salmon and the others would have to leave the valley. Jackson would take it from them, would not hesitate to kill them all if necessary. And if Jackson hesitated, Larrabee would not. Larrabee had a personal score to settle with Gabe, and if, in the process, he had a chance to kill a couple dozen Indians, he would count that a bonus.

Gabe's continued presence was an actual danger to Spotted Fawn's people.

The first people he told were Spotted Fawn and Salmon. Salmon reacted angrily. "I will not leave!" he cried out.

Spotted Fawn reasoned with him. "To stay is to die," she said. "And there has been enough dying."

The word went around the village. There were two days of arguments and despair. Some wanted to stay and fight, some wanted to leave. Gabe took no part in the discussions. His mind was already elsewhere.

It was Spotted Fawn who told him about the village's decision. "We will go back to the reservation," she said. "There, life is hard, but with the army near, there is a chance that we might survive."

Gabe nodded. "You and I, then," he said, "we'll go away together. I will take you to places where we can live in peace."

To his surprise, Spotted Fawn shook her head. "I will go with my people. That is the life I know."

She hesitated. "I am going to have a child, Gabe. Your child, but I want that child to grow up among the people with whom I grew up."

Gabe studied the girl for quite a while. Yes, she had that look about her, of a woman with a child inside her belly. Along with that look, she had gained a new maturity.

"I will not go to the reservation," he said.

She nodded her head slowly. "I know. And I am very sad. But . . . the child . . ."

She reached out a hand, touched him gently. There was, indeed, great sadness in her eyes. But also, purpose. "It was not to be," she said softly. "You and I. It was not to last forever."

He took her hand. "No. It was not."

• • •

The next few days were filled with a sadness that was, in its own way, not unpleasant. Finally, the entire village was ready for the move. It would take them more than a day to walk back to the reservation. Gabe would not go along with them. He would ride out alone. He stood by his horse, all his gear on its back. His good-byes had been said the night before. Along with his good-byes, he had given Spotted Fawn the last of his money.

A few yards away, Spotted Fawn was helping an old woman pick up some of her belongings. Gabe mounted. Spotted Fawn saw the movement, looked up. Their eyes met. He saw a moment's flicker of pain, of loss, in the girl's eyes. Saw love. Saw, also, her new sense of determination, and he knew that if Spotted Fawn survived, she would do well. As would the child she was carrying. His child.

Once again, he thought about staying, then discarded the idea. As he had already realized, his continued presence, with so many of the local settlers seeking revenge against him, would only endanger the tribe.

So, with a wave, he rode away, turning in the saddle once to see Spotted Fawn looking after him intently. Then, as the trees closed around him, he saw her no more.

He rode straight toward the reservation. It took him most of the morning, but eventually he saw buildings ahead. Riding to a point a few hundred yards from the reservation headquarters, he tied up his horse. Taking his binoculars from his saddlebags, he settled down to wait and watch.

An hour later he saw Broaddus come out the door, then walk off toward the Indian village. Ghosting through the trees, Gabe approached the building. It was easy to slip inside, unseen.

Broaddus came back an hour later. Gabe heard him walk in the door, apparently alone, which was good, or Gabe might have had to kill someone. Gabe was sitting in a chair when Broaddus walked into the room. It was gloomy inside the room, and Broaddus did not at first see him. He moved about the room absentmindedly, whistling tunelessly. Then he finally became aware that he was not alone. Broaddus was standing sideways to Gabe's chair. Gabe saw the other man's shoulders tense. Broaddus turned slowly, as if he would rather not. "You!" he gasped.

Gabe stood up slowly. He noticed that Broaddus was staring at the pistol on his hip. There was terror in his eyes. "What . . . what do you want?" he asked.

Gabe walked up to him. Broaddus shrank back. "There will be some people coming here," Gabe said, his voice flat, deadly. "They intend to live among the others already here. They are people who once left this place, because you let them starve. They are people I care about."

He said nothing for several seconds, then added, "If you do anything to harm those people, Broaddus, I will kill you. I will come back here and kill you. And if I do not find you here, I will follow wherever you have gone, and then I will kill you."

Broaddus seemed unable to reply. Gabe pinned him with his eyes for a moment longer, then turned and left the room.

When he had remounted his horse he thought about riding east, through the mountains. But there were other things to do. Before he left this land, he must go to Eureka. He must let it be known that he was leaving. But he must also make certain that there would be those who would fear his possible return.

He took a leisurely two days to travel to Eureka. He rode in late the next afternoon. He went straight to the offices of the lumber company and asked to see Jackson. A clerk, slowly beginning to realize who this stranger was, this man with the cold eyes, wearing a long black coat with some kind of bird painted on the back, grew very nervous. "He . . . he's not here," the clerk stammered. "He . . . had to go back East, on b-business."

Gabe suspected that the clerk was telling the truth. Too bad. He would have liked to meet Jackson, would have liked to study a man so greedy that he would hire a killer like Larrabee to massacre innocent people just because they stood in the way of his greater profit.

Gabe turned, looked out the window. He saw a huge building about a quarter of a mile away, in the final stages of construction. It was the largest building in sight. He remembered something Dugan had told him. "Is that Jackson's new house?" he asked the clerk,

"Uh . . . yessir."

Gabe studied the house a while longer. An extravaganza of soaring towers, bay windows, and masses of gingerbread decoration. The house that greed built.

He left the office without another word. Now it was time to find Larrabee. He was not in town, either, but, unlike Jackson, he was not very far away. Gabe discovered, from a nervous man he questioned on the street, that Larrabee was presently living on a ranch about twenty miles away.

Gabe left town, then spent the rest of the day in the woods. Shortly after dark he rode back toward town. His approach took him close to Jackson's new house. The workmen had gone home for the night. Gabe was not challenged as he rode up to the house. It took him only a little while to find a store of kerosene. He poured it liberally all over the ground floor. He stood in the doorway, struck a match with his fingernail, then threw it inside. He waited a minute, watching the first flames lick upward. Suddenly, a sheet of fire darted toward the stairwell with a loud whoosh. Mounting his horse, Gabe rode away toward the main road. A few hundred yards further along, he turned to look back at the house. Already, flames were shooting out of some of the windows.

Gabe spent the night in the woods. At dawn, he began searching for Larrabee's place. It was not difficult to find. Gabe approached it not long after the sun rose. It was a smallish ranch, located in a broad valley, near a large river. Good land. However, the ranch buildings were not impressive. Gabe had expected to find a lot of people around Larrabee, but, to his surprise, he saw only one man, an old hostler, who, despite the early hour, was already busy in the corral.

The hostler had not yet seen Gabe, so he rode into a thicket and dismounted, not far from the ranch house. It was not long before he saw Larrabee himself, walking out the front door, heading toward the outhouse. Larrabee was not quite fully dressed; he was wearing suspenders over the tops of long johns tucked into dirty trousers. He was also wearing boots and a pistol.

Gabe waited until Larrabee had used the outhouse. He was standing in the open when Larrabee came back outside. The house itself screened both of them from the hostler's view.

Larrabee, scratching under his armpits, slammed the outhouse door behind him, perhaps thinking of breakfast. Then he saw Gabe. He stopped abruptly, as if he'd run into something hard. His hands fluttered uselessly, but Gabe noticed that he kept his right hand away from the butt of his pistol.

"I understand you're looking for me," Gabe said.

"I, uhhhh . . ."

"I understand you are willing to take money to wipe out a village full of peaceful people."

When Larrabee did not reply, Gabe said, "But then . . . I suppose if there were no money involved, you'd kill them anyhow, just for the fun of it."

Larrabee finally found his voice. "I . . . I got no fight with you, mister."

"Oh, I'm afraid you do," Gabe replied.

His voice hardened. "And that fight is right now."

"No, I . . ."

Larrabee was backing away, toward the outhouse, his hands out in front of him. A coward, as before, Gabe thought. A man who liked hacking women and children to death with hatchets. One who would not face an armed opponent whom he knew was capable of killing him.

But Larrabee had read the implacable purpose in Gabe's eyes, knew that nothing he could do would stop Gabe from fighting him. Gabe read that awareness in Larrabee's eyes and was prepared when Larrabee made his move. Pretending to stumble, Larrabee bent low, his left hand braced on the ground. He was partly crouched, using the fake fall as a screen, while his right hand moved toward the butt of his pistol.

Both men drew together. Larrabee was still in a crouch, which made him a more difficult target. Both men fired almost together, but Gabe's first shot got off a split second earlier, early enough so that when the bullet struck Larrabee low in the chest, it ruined Larrabee's aim. His bullet flew wide of Gabe.

Gabe had drawn with his left hand. Now he wrapped both hands around the butt of the pistol. Holding back the trigger with his left index finger, he worked the hammer with his right thumb, pistol out ahead, firmly held, aimed straight at Larrabee. He emptied the five remaining shots into Larrabee's body, driving him back against the outhouse, which swayed and almost fell.

Larrabee slid down the side of the outhouse, leaving long smears of blood on the weathered boards. None of the shots that had hit him had brought instant death, but death was not far off. He sat, propped against the outhouse wall, legs straight out in front of him, pistol still in his hand, looking down with horror at the blood bubbling from his chest and stomach. He tried to look up at Gabe, his head rising jerkily. But he didn't make it. The last of his life left him; his head dropped down onto his shattered breast. Larrabee would slaughter no more helpless women and children.

Gabe felt no sense of triumph as he looked down at Larrabee's dead body. He felt only a desire to get out of there, to get out of the entire area. To leave this Eden of death far behind him.

He heard the hostler yelling, heard booted feet heading in his direction. But Gabe had already mounted, was riding away into the brush, giving the hostler one brief glimpse of the Thunderbird painted on the back of his coat. Gabe wanted it that way, wanted it known who had killed Larrabee.

He rode south, following the river. A high wall of mountains lay ahead. They might not be easy to cross, but he would cross them. Perhaps, if he rode far enough south, he would find that land he had heard about, the land where winter never comes.

But as he rode, an image formed in his mind. An image of dark, soft eyes. An image of a young woman dressed in a short deerskin skirt. An image of a young woman who had once been his woman, but whom he would not see again. A woman who had made the right decision, for Gabe knew that his life was destined to be a lonely life, a ceaseless wandering. The life of a man lost between two worlds.

A life that would be his until the day he died.

If you enjoyed this book, subscribe now and get...

TWO FREE

A $7.00 VALUE—

If you would like to read more of the very best, most exciting, adventurous, action-packed Westerns being published today, you'll want to subscribe to True Value's Western Home Subscription Service.

Each month the editors of True Value will select the 6 very best Westerns from America's leading publishers for special readers like you. You'll be able to preview these new titles as soon as they are published, *FREE* for ten days with no obligation!

TWO FREE BOOKS

When you subscribe, we'll send you your first month's shipment of the newest and best 6 Westerns for you to preview. With your first shipment, two of these books will be yours as our introductory gift to you absolutely *FREE* (a $7.00 value), regardless of what you decide to do. If

you like them, as much as we think you will, keep all six books but pay for just 4 at the low subscriber rate of just $2.75 each. If you decide to return them, keep 2 of the titles as our gift. No obligation.

Special Subscriber Savings

When you become a True Value subscriber you'll save money several ways. First, all regular monthly selections will be billed at the low subscriber price of just $2.75 each. That's at least a savings of $4.50 each month below the publishers price. Second, there is never any shipping, handling or other hidden charges—*Free home delivery*. What's more there is no minimum number of books you must buy, you may return any selection for full credit and you can cancel your subscription at any time. A TRUE VALUE!

WESTERNS!

NO OBLIGATION

Mail the coupon below

To start your subscription and receive 2 FREE WESTERNS, fill out the coupon below and mail it today. We'll send your first shipment which includes 2 FREE BOOKS as soon as we receive it.

Mail To: **True Value Home Subscription Services, Inc. P.O. Box 5235**
120 Brighton Road, Clifton, New Jersey 07015-5235

YES! I want to start reviewing the very best Westerns being published today. Send me my first shipment of 6 Westerns for me to preview FREE for 10 days. If I decide to keep them, I'll pay for just 4 of the books at the low subscriber price of $2.75 each; a total $11.00 (a $21.00 value). Then each month I'll receive the 6 newest and best Westerns to preview Free for 10 days. If I'm not satisfied I may return them within 10 days and owe nothing. Otherwise I'll be billed at the special low subscriber rate of $2.75 each; a total of $16.50 (at least a $21.00 value) and save $4.50 off the publishers price. There are never any shipping, handling or other hidden charges. I understand I am under no obligation to purchase any number of books and I can cancel my subscription at any time, no questions asked. In any case the 2 FREE books are mine to keep.

Name _____

Street Address _____ Apt. No. _____

City _____ State _____ Zip Code _____

Telephone _____

Signature _____
(if under 18 parent or guardian must sign)

919-6

Terms and prices subject to change. Orders subject
to acceptance by True Value Home Subscription
Services, Inc.